TH
HALTI

by

STEVEN A. McKAY

Copyright © 2024
All rights reserved. No part of this book may be reproduced,
in whole or in part, without prior written permission
from the copyright holder.

Dedicated to my big mate Bil Moore.

ONE

November, c. AD 1330.
EAST YORKSHIRE

"Why do you test me so, Father?" The man on the palfrey sighed deeply and glanced up at the sky as heavy drops of icy rain began to fall. From the look of the clouds it was not to be a quick shower he and his mount would be subjected to and he groaned inwardly as those first few droplets quickly turned into a deluge.

Kicking his heels in, the rider headed off the side of the road to shelter beneath a copse of trees that were luckily nearby. The rain was already dripping from the hood of his grey robe by the time the horse pulled up beneath the spreading branches of a sweet chestnut tree. He realised his earlier admonishment of the Almighty was misplaced – at least God had saved this downpour until he was close to shelter. The rain practically thundered off the ground and he was thankful for the meagre foliage that remained on the tree for it did just enough to keep him relatively dry as he and the palfrey hugged the chestnut's hoary trunk.

"Forgive me, Father," he murmured, clasping his hands and closing his eyes to make suitable penance for his poor grace. When he looked out again at the rolling fields around him he was struck by the barren, eerie feel of the place. Robert Stafford, or Friar Tuck as he'd been known for years now, had travelled extensively in his fifty plus years, had once been a member of the infamous outlaw Robin Hood's gang, and had faced many dangerous enemies, some of which might even have been demonic in nature. Before his life as a churchman he'd been a successful wrestler and even now, at a shade under six feet tall, he could wield a staff with greater skill and brutality than most soldiers. In short, Tuck was not a man to be easily spooked, and especially not by the sight of a bit of late-autumn countryside.

Still, as the rain finally began to ease and a hint of sunlight cast an almost ethereal orange glow on the road ahead, the friar could not suppress a shudder. There was something odd about his surroundings and he resolved to press his mount a little harder that they might reach their destination as soon as possible.

"Come on then, girl," he said kindly to the palfrey, urging it out from the shelter of the trees. "Not far to go now I think."

He did not even need to push the animal for it trotted quicker than it had been doing before the shower: apparently it too had sensed something of the ill-omened nature of the place. A few cows were in a nearby field and even they seemed oddly malevolent as they eyed the friar riding past.

Pushing aside his wilder flights of fancy, Tuck focused his gaze on the road that stretched before them and pondered the reason for his journey.

An old acquaintance from the days when Tuck had become a friar had written asking if Tuck might pay him a visit at the newly founded Haltemprice Priory in Newton, East Yorkshire, where he had taken up a position as cantor. It seemed an odd request for, although they had been friends, they had not been in touch for many years and Tuck was a Franciscan friar while his friend was a Benedictine monk. Why either man would wish to meet again was a mystery to Tuck. Still, he lived in Wakefield now and that was only about fifty miles from Haltemprice Priory so, intrigued, Tuck decided to answer the call and make the journey.

Simon de Poher had been an unremarkable young man, Tuck remembered. Average in height, gaunt, with small features, he fitted in well with the other monks for he caused no trouble. Tuck had been older, and had experienced far more in life, being employed after his wrestling days as a bodyguard for much higher-ranking clergymen of various orders. He had found de Poher pleasant enough on the occasions they encountered one another, and sometimes one even sought out the other for conversation and learning.

Tuck had moved on from that life and, as the years passed he rarely thought of the nondescript young monk. Tuck remembered him fondly now, but he knew next to nothing about what Simon de Poher had been doing with his life recently, or about the priory at Haltemprice.

The rain, which had stopped some miles back, began once more, a persistent smirr that seeped into one's very bones, making Tuck shiver. He would be happy when he reached the priory and could dry himself by a roaring fire with a mug of ale in his hand. That thought cheered him: churchmen, the higher-ranking ones at least, knew how to live, and how to welcome a guest. There would be decent food and drink at Haltemprice Priory, and Tuck liked few things in life better than a good meal.

Yet as he shook the rain from his hood and took in the gloomy heath he was traversing now, he wondered just exactly what he might be letting himself in for this dreary November.

TWO

It was dry by the time Tuck's tired palfrey brought him to Haltemprice Priory, but the atmosphere in the surrounding countryside had only grown heavier and more oppressive as their journey neared its end. The friar could not remember ever feeling anything like it before – as if the very air itself was reaching out to attack him with grasping fingers. He knew that was a ridiculous notion, but he could not shake it and when he saw the priory itself his mood did not lift as he'd hoped.

The place was quite magnificent in the late afternoon gloom, the dying sun framing it in red-orange so it almost looked as if it was aflame. The bell tower drew the eye first, dominating the landscape with its height and bulk, but the rest of the buildings adjoining it – church, chapter house, infirmary, and cloisters – were no less impressive with their myriad glazed windows. There were other structures Tuck took to be the bakehouse, brewery, guest houses, and even a mill, and the whole complex spread out across a large area.

The friar had, of course, seen many such sites over the years, but Haltemprice was very new, its massive stone walls commanding the area around it like some…Tuck suppressed a shudder at the strange similes that came to mind as he took in the sight of the forbidding priory that would be his home for the next few days. Now that he looked closer, he could see that some sections of the complex were still under construction, as scaffolding, cranes, and building supplies surrounded certain areas.

A sudden gust of wind buffeted him, blowing through a gap in a nearby tree and making a low piping sound that startled Tuck so badly that his hand fell to the cudgel at his waist. Chuckling in embarrassment he left the weapon alone and tried, again, to calm himself. He was being foolish, that much was obvious, but he wished one of his friends was with him at that moment. John Little, or Will Scaflock perhaps. He'd known both since his time with Robin Hood, and they remained close friends with the friar.

Those two were warriors however, and there was no earthly danger around – what Tuck was afraid of was something far less tangible than robbers or even some extreme weather. What it might be he couldn't say, but he did wonder if the feeling of dread that had grown within him these past few miles had something to do with why Simon de Poher had asked him to visit.

A wolf howled from a hilltop in the distance, making the friar's mount skittish, but they were close to the priory now and the sound urged them onwards, the wind picking up behind them and almost carrying them along.

The gates were open and Tuck rode through, casting about for a place to leave the palfrey. He spotted the stables immediately and a fresh-faced novice appeared from one of the stalls.

"Brother Tuck?" the youth asked shortly. "I was told you'd be here sometime. I've got a place ready for your horse."

Tuck dismounted and took his belongings from the saddlebag. He smiled at the stableboy but his only reply was a pensive frown as the youngster took the reins and led the horse away to be rubbed down and made comfortable for the coming night.

"Where do I go now?" Tuck called.

With the barest glance over his shoulder the lad pointed towards the enormous main doors and said, "In there, brother."

Tuck sighed and headed for the entrance. The stableboy had not been rude or belligerent, but neither had he been friendly, which was unusual. People in such professions generally went out of their way to be overly helpful in hopes of receiving a coin or two. Something was bothering the youth, that much was certain, and it simply added to the heavy sense of oppression building within Tuck.

The doors were barred from within and he thumped his fist against them, irritated and surprised by the poor welcome. Priories were usually busy places, yet this one seemed as silent as the tomb. When his thumping wasn't answered he drew out the cudgel from beneath his robe and rapped it sharply against the door.

Moments later a voice called out from within, "Who's there?"

"It's Brother Tuck, from Wakefield!"

The clattering of bolts drawing back filtered through to him and then one of the pair of doors was opened to reveal Tuck's old friend, Simon de Poher.

"Tuck!" the black-robed cantor said with an obviously relieved yet wan smile. "Come in, brother. I apologise for this less than warm welcome. Come in, come in." He stepped back, features settling into a more relaxed and happy expression as the tall, sturdy friar came through the doors into the priory.

"Good to see you again, Simon," Tuck said honestly, pleased at their reunion but intrigued by the excessively hollow features and darting eyes of his old acquaintance. What the hell was wrong with the people here in Haltemprice Priory?

De Poher stared at him for a few heartbeats, almost looking right through him, but then he shook himself visibly and fixed the smile back onto his narrow face. "Come, my friend," he said. "I'll show you to your quarters."

At this point Tuck would normally have made some light-hearted remark about the level of luxury he hoped to enjoy during his stay at the priory, but he sensed such jocularity would be ill-received and he kept his mouth shut as he was led to the right and past the dormitory. "You'll not be sleeping in there with the monks," de Poher said, instead opening the door to a little room that held a bed, a chair, and a desk. "As a guest, you have a cell to yourself."

There was a window which let in the little daylight that remained and Tuck nodded, happy enough. He'd seen worse accommodation in his life as a churchman. This looked comfortable and would shelter him from the worst of the wind that had picked up since he'd arrived there in Haltemprice.

"Thank you," he said to de Poher who bowed his head in acknowledgement. "I appreciate having this space of my own."

"Oh, it's much nicer than sharing a communal dormitory," the de Poher agreed quietly. "I have my own private cell too – a perk of being cantor. Anyway, Tuck, I'll give you some time to settle in, and then I'll take you to the refectory for refreshments. You must be hungry and thirsty from your journey."

For the first time in hours Tuck felt his spirits rise. Meat and drink always cheered him up. "Thank you," he said, and de Poher left, closing the door behind him.

Tuck sat on the bed and closed his eyes, breathing in and out slowly, just letting the quiet wash over him and soothe away the unease he'd felt on the road. He realised now that the priory was not as silent as he'd first thought – he could hear low voices and footsteps all around him, vague metallic noises and thuds probably from monks working and digging in the gardens outside his window, and the general hubbub of a working priory that was still under construction in some places. The sounds definitely seemed subdued though, as if the monks were afraid of being too loud. While those noises should have been homely and set Tuck at ease, here in Haltemprice their muffled tones merely served to rouse his anxiety even further. He was also somewhat surprised by the fact that Simon de Poher had his own cell – usually the brothers all shared a communal dormitory as originally decreed in the Rule of St Benedict in the 6th century. Still, lots of things had changed in the intervening centuries and every prior or abbot had their own vision on how things should be done – it was not Tuck's place to question that, no matter how unusual things seemed.

When he opened his eyes Tuck was amazed to find that night had drawn in faster than he'd expected, or perhaps more clouds had simply swept in to blanket the sun, for it was quite dark within the cell already.

He knelt beside the bed and murmured a soft prayer of thanks for the safe completion of his journey and then, moving carefully in the gloom, he washed his face in the bowl of water that had been left out for him, drying off with a fresh towel that the priory's guest-master must have also provided.

There was a candle on the table and Tuck thought about lighting it but before he could there came a tap on the door and de Poher's face appeared, pale and strained.

"Are you ready?" the cantor asked.

"For food?" Tuck replied, perhaps with excessive jocularity. "Always. Lead on, brother!"

THREE

On the way to the refectory they passed through the cloister. Tonsured, black-robed monks were hard at work here in the arcaded, straw-covered walks, with novices learning the complicated forms of service and rules of the priory on the western side, while older men studied and produced books by hand in the north walk. Tuck was amazed by the work of the illuminator in particular, a middle-aged man with slim fingers and keen eyes who was employed at that moment in painting a vibrant scene depicting a group of noblemen beside a fountain. As Brother de Poher led him on, they passed scribes copying out texts including entire bibles, while rubricators added colourful titles and initial letters to volumes that would likely take years to complete. Although it was very quiet, the cloister was a veritable hive of activity.

They reached the refectory and, upon entering, Tuck saw it was, like the rest of the priory complex, newly built and freshly decorated. The friar gazed around as they sat at one of the long benches and nodded approvingly.

"I'm impressed," he told the cantor. "The builders are doing a good job."

"So they should be," de Poher said. "They're being paid enough, or so the steward keeps telling anyone who'll listen." He rolled his eyes. "They've stopped work for now although I'm not sure why. Some lord's manor house needed to be completed or something like that I imagine. Something else for the steward to moan about."

Tuck chuckled. Complaining stewards were ubiquitous within church properties. A gust of wind buffeted the windows though, and the friar raised his eyebrows. "Just as well you have had good builders," he noted. "If that wind is always so violent."

De Poher's reply was little more than a grunt but his expression was drawn and he eyed the windows almost fearfully. Tuck was beginning to feel as though he was a character in some winter ghost story, like the ones about witches and the undead recorded centuries before by Ælfric of Eynsham.

A young boy appeared from the kitchen carrying a trencher of bread, cheese, and roast beef in a rich sauce of some local recipe. He set it down gingerly as if he'd dropped something on an earlier occasion and wanted to make sure the spill was not repeated. Undoubtedly, he'd have had a good clip around the ear from the cook for his clumsiness but he managed his task and hurried off, returning quickly with a jug of ale and a pair of cups. Tuck thanked the boy, who didn't meet his eyes or acknowledge him in any way before disappearing once more.

The food was tasty – much tastier than Tuck had expected in fact. He'd feared the beef would be as bland and uninspiring as the atmosphere in the priory but it was soft and tender, and the sauce was bursting with peppery flavour. He ate with gusto, washing it all down with two cups of ale which, again, was delicious.

De Poher drank a little but did not eat, and neither man spoke during the meal, as was the rule in

Haltemprice, but Tuck was so famished that he thought nothing of it and, in fact, didn't even register the whining and rattling of the wind until he'd finished and sat back patting his ample belly.

"Did you enjoy that?"

"I did," the friar agreed heartily. "But perhaps we should find somewhere less draughty and you can tell me why you invited me here."

A shadow flitted across the cantor's face but he nodded and got to his feet, gesturing towards the door. Tuck led the way but the cantor passed him in the cloister and they headed east, past the chapter house, the wind buffeting them until they made it to the library and de Poher closed the door.

It was dark within, the chamber lit only by the last vestiges of daylight coming through the window set high in the rear wall. Bringing a candle from the refectory would obviously have been pointless for the wind in the cloisters would have quickly extinguished its flame, but Tuck spotted another near the door. Within moments he had taken out his flint and steel and used them to bring the candle to life, the heady scent of beeswax filling the air.

"I've never seen anyone light a candle so fast!" de Poher observed with some surprise.

"You learn a lot when you're forced to live as an outlaw in the greenwood," said the friar, carefully packing away his equipment and making sure his tinder was fully extinguished. Of all the places one might accidentally start a fire, the priory library would be one of the worst.

"Please, brother, sit."

Tuck looked around, impressed by the collection of scrolls and books within the compact library, then he did as he was bidden and eased his bulky frame down on one of the nearby chairs.

The cantor took a seat across from him and eyed him seriously for a moment. Now that it was time to get down to the business at hand it seemed as if he was reluctant to talk; he swallowed, rubbed his tonsured head, and licked his lips. Tuck decided to speak first, fearing they'd be locked in the library all night if he didn't.

"This is a very impressive priory," he said, peering up and gesturing vaguely around, his hand casting long shadows in the candlelight. "I'd have thought the brothers and lay people living here would be happy with their new surroundings."

"And yet…" Simon de Poher breathed, chewing his lip.

"And yet." Tuck nodded. "I've hardly seen anyone so far, as if everyone is hiding, and those I have met seem nervous about something. Frightened even."

The door to the cloister rattled at his words, pushed against the latch by the gusting wind outside.

De Poher swallowed again and looked up at the ceiling, as if he were begging God for guidance.

Tuck stood and walked to the nearest bookcase. He knew some of the library's collection was valuable as some of the books were actually chained to the shelves so they could not be lost or stolen. The shelves themselves were brand new and had clearly been made by skilled carpenters, but many of the books on show were very old and Tuck hesitated to draw any out in case he damaged them.

"You're right," de Poher said behind him. "Everyone in Haltemprice seems to be anxious, including me."

"Why?" Tuck asked, turning back to face him.

"Well, that's the thing," the cantor chuckled bleakly. "I have no idea."

Tuck's brow lifted and he leaned back thoughtfully. "You must have some clue," he stated.

"No," the cantor said, shaking his head. "Nothing has happened as far as I'm aware. No one has died violently, or threatened us, or, well, anything like that at all in the time that we've been here. This place..." He trailed off, casting wary glances into the dark corners and at one particular section of books. "This place just seems to crush the spirit, which is unfathomable given it's a house of God!" He cringed as he said the last few words, as if fearing he'd be struck down by a divine bolt of lightning or, perhaps, something less holy...

"I do understand what you mean," Tuck told him, moving towards the bookcases again, this time heading for the shelf that had drawn de Poher's nervous gaze moments before. "I felt it even on the road here. There's something strangely oppressive about the whole area. You think it's focused on Haltemprice itself?"

The cantor visibly shivered. It seemed he hadn't thought of that until now. "I'm not sure," he murmured. "Maybe something bad happened here in the distant past, before the priory was built. Echoes of it are still being felt through time or... something." He trailed off and rubbed his shaved head self-consciously, sweating despite the chilly air in the library.

Tuck looked at the books on the shelf before him and felt a sudden twinge of recognition. He'd seen, and even skimmed through, some of these ancient tomes a few years before, in the collection owned by Father Nicholas de Nottingham, priest of St Mary's in Brandesburton. *Cultes de Goules*, *De Vermis Mysteriis*, and *Liber Os Abysmi vel Daath*.

"Strange volumes to be held in a priory's library," Tuck noted, glancing at de Poher before gingerly drawing out one that was chained to the shelf. Named *The Black Book of Azathoth*, Tuck opened it at a random page before shuddering and hurriedly returning it.

"They belong to my friend," said the cantor, not surprised by Tuck's reaction to the blasphemous tome. "Edward Magnus. He's the cellarer here at Haltemprice."

"I'd like to meet him," Tuck said, although he was thinking the exact opposite. Surely any man whose reading material was as sinister as *The Black Book of Azathoth* was to be avoided! Then again, Father de Nottingham in Brandesburton had been a kind, God-fearing fellow who merely used his collection of occult texts to learn how to combat the evils that assailed mankind – perhaps Edward Magnus did the same.

"Yes," de Poher agreed. "You should meet him. Perhaps he can help you discover what's afflicting the priory and its environs."

"Help me what?" Tuck laughed in astonishment. "Is that why you invited me here? You want me to investigate a problem that seems to have no earthly cause or, indeed, solution?"

De Poher nodded vigorously. "Yes, old friend. Who better? We've all heard of your exploits in recent years, solving strange mysteries and catching vicious, heretical criminals. I suggested we invite you here, and Prior Engayne agreed. You must help, Tuck, we have no one else to turn to. Prayers do not help!"

The friar stared at him, wondering if this was all some elaborate joke, but the fear and desperation on Simon de Poher's gaunt face was no act. The man had always been a nervous soul, but he was practically crippled with anxiety now.

With a heavy sigh, Tuck nodded. "Very well. Let's find this cellarer, Edward Magnus, and hear what he has to say about all this."

FOUR

"Where are we going?" Tuck asked as de Poher led him to a doorway that opened onto a descending flight of stairs.

"To see Edward in the undercroft," the cantor replied, not slowing as he went down. "Take care, these steps can get slippery. At least we'll not hear the gale down here, since there's no windows. It's quite cosy actually, if you don't mind it being dark even during daytime."

Cosy? Tuck thought in amazement. It was true the wind did not blow so hard along the corridor as they headed for wherever it was de Poher was taking them, but it was damp, gloomy, and smelled oddly fusty. Tuck suspected the cellar and undercroft might have been here for aeons – certainly long before the priory was built over them. They were anything but cosy!

"Why would anyone want to spend time down here?" he wondered, eyes scanning the impenetrable shadows of open rooms they passed. He half expected demons to come pouring out of those gaping black doorways, lit only by the feeble glow of the lantern that de Poher had brought with them.

"Oh, Edward likes to keep himself to himself," the cantor said. "So he can be found down here often, just reading his books and praying."

Tuck understood that. Many Christians enjoyed solitude, believing they could better commune with God in private places like this, undisturbed by chattering novices or demanding superiors. Still, he couldn't help but feel on edge in the dreary space beneath the new building.

"Ah, look," de Poher whispered. Somehow it seemed natural to lower one's voice in the undercroft. "Light. Edward must be down here."

Tuck peered over the cantor's shoulder as they walked. Sure enough, a flickering orange glow spilled out from a room at the far end of the passageway and they soon reached it. The fusty smell was much stronger here, overpowering even the beeswax from the candle and almost making Tuck retch for there was something…meaty to it, that set the hairs on his neck rising.

As de Poher predicted, in the chamber was a man who looked at them as they came through the open door. Tuck examined him, seeing a narrow-faced, goatish individual in the dim light cast by a couple of candles and a lantern. The room did not have much in it but in one dark corner the friar saw a strange metallic apparatus, with tubes and containers all constructed from bronze or copper the like of which Tuck had never seen or even heard of before.

"Brother Magnus!" the cantor said, a sickly smile playing across his hollow features. He stopped some distance away from the cellarer, fiddling with his hands as though he felt even more nervous than he had before coming down here.

Edward Magnus was visibly irritated by the interruption and he cast de Poher a black look before turning his piercing stare on Tuck who returned the look coolly.

"Who's this?" the cellarer drawled, closing the book he'd been reading. Tuck tried to make out the title of the heavy volume, only managing to catch the first part of it, *Necro-* something or other. A Latin word meaning 'the dead'.

"Oh, this is an old friend of mine," de Poher blurted, smiling at the cellarer in an ingratiating way that Tuck found quite distasteful. Why was he so desperate to please, or impress, the other man? Was it simply because the cellarer was his superior? Or was there something else behind the cantor's fawning behaviour? "Brother Tuck. A Franciscan, from Wakefield," de Poher continued, oblivious to the friar's critical gaze.

"Ah, I remember now," Magnus muttered, getting to his feet in a way that reminded Tuck of a spider, unfolding long limbs and seeming to dominate the gloomy little chamber. Friar Tuck was tall at just under six feet, but Edward Magnus loomed over him, standing completely still, like a hunter waiting for its prey.

"He hopes to find out why Haltemprice feels so…cursed," de Poher said, voice trailing off as he spoke the final word.

"Is that so?" Magnus said, eyes boring into Tuck as if the cellarer might read his very thoughts. A lesser man, like de Poher, might have wilted under the intense gaze, but Tuck had dealt with plenty of fearsome individuals in his time.

"Perhaps," the friar replied, feeling like a wolf facing a rival for the honour of leading the pack. "I'll certainly try. I find these unusual mysteries interesting."

"So you do," Magnus agreed with a laugh. "I've heard all about your adventures. You captured a dangerous heretic not so long ago, didn't you? Well done, brother. Can't have heretics spreading their poison around England, can we?"

Tuck accepted the praise gratefully, although the smile that played about the cellarer's mouth had more than a hint of mockery in it, or so the friar imagined.

"Where are your friends? William Scaflock is it? And the prodigiously tall one that people humorously call Little John?"

At that moment Tuck wished Scaflock was with him. Nicknamed 'Scarlet' for his effervescent, explosive temper, Will would have put this preening peacock firmly in his place, probably minus a tooth or three. Tuck was more civilised, however, and he replied, "Maybe they'll join me later, depending on what I find here."

Magnus appeared genuinely amused by the thought, but he guided the conversation in a different direction, asking, "What brings you down here to visit me, brother?" as he stroked his neat grey goatee.

"I noticed the shelf in the library," Tuck said, watching his sparring partner for any reaction to his words. "The one where you keep your esoteric book collection."

"Esoteric," Magnus said, mocking smile not wavering. "Yes, I like that description. What of it? I enjoy reading volumes of hidden knowledge. Like this one." He pointed at the book he'd been poring over when Tuck and de Poher first came into the room. "The *Necronomicon*. Written, so they say, by a madman in some exotic eastern land. Truly a fascinating read."

"And you believe you might find something in there, or in the books chained up in the library above, that might help you fight off whatever evil is assailing Haltemprice?" Tuck asked.

Magnus snorted. It seemed he was thoroughly enjoying this encounter with the legendary friar who so many stories and songs had been written about over the years. "Yes," he returned happily. "That's exactly right, Brother Tuck. I search occult books for ways to fight evil."

"Any luck so far?" Tuck asked, not liking the cellarer's tone at all.

Shrugging, Edward Magnus turned away and sat down, picking up the dread *Necronomicon* once again. It fell open to the same page the cellarer had been reading earlier, as though Magnus had read, and reread, that section multiple times. Tuck wished he could see what was on those particular pages but, if it was anything like he'd found in *The Black Book of Azathoth*, he'd probably be better off not knowing.

"No, no luck," the cellarer replied. "Perhaps I will have a breakthrough today, or tomorrow. Perhaps never."

There was silence then as friar and cellarer gazed coolly at one another, as though vying for supremacy. It was clear the meeting was close to an end, but Tuck did not want to leave before he found out what the odd metal equipment in the corner was for.

"What's that, brother?" he asked, pointing at the tubes and crucibles.

Magnus glanced into the corner and his expression grew secretive. "Just something I use for my experiments. It's designed along the same lines as the apparatus used by the alchemist, Maria the Prophetess. Have you heard of her? Sometimes she's known as Maria the Jewess."

Reluctantly, Tuck shook his head.

"Why does that not surprise me?" the cellarer said with a sneer. "Now," he waved a hand as though he were dismissing some serving wench in a seedy tavern. "Leave me. I must work."

Simon de Poher seemed utterly oblivious to the cellarer's rudeness, and he held out his hands, ushering Tuck towards the door. The friar was only too happy to leave the fetid room with its odious occupant and gladly headed along the passageway to the stairs that would take them mercifully back to the cloisters and fresh air.

They walked in silence and Tuck pondered the strange meeting with Edward Magnus. As they went out into the cloisters and the wind assailed them once more the friar suddenly realised the one thing that had disturbed him more than any other about the cellarer – Edward Magnus, in contrast with everyone else Tuck had seen so far at Haltemprice Priory, seemed happy.

FIVE

Tuck did not sleep at all well that night. The bed was soft enough, that was true, and the cell was comfortable, but the wind did not relent, constantly pushing against the single small window so he feared it would eventually give way and allow the shrieking gale within. Why that worried him so much the friar could not rightly say, but the few hours of sleep he was able to snatch were troubled, and filled with frightening dreams Tuck could thankfully not recall when dawn finally called the inhabitants of Haltemprice from their beds for another day's work and prayer.

It had been quite some years since Tuck had lived amongst a religious order like the Benedictines there in the priory – he'd almost forgotten just how early they rose in the mornings. Some priors and abbots still held to the old ways, forcing their monks to get up soon after midnight to walk to Mattins in the freezing, candlelit church, where the circator would walk around them, shining his lantern in the face of any who dared fall asleep during the service.

Blearily, Tuck washed the sleep from his face, and cleaned his teeth with a frayed birch twig, giving thanks that Prior Engayne allowed the brethren here to rest until dawn. Then, somewhat refreshed, the friar went out to join the rest of the community in breaking their fast before Prime.

Simon de Poher was there to greet Tuck outside his cell and they walked to the refectory complaining about how the wind continued to rattle the doors and windows of the priory making it difficult to sleep.

There was porridge and ale in the bustling refectory and Tuck grabbed the chance to examine the monks. They seemed, to a man, to be subdued and even sullen, ignoring the friar's smile of greeting.

"Ah, Brother Tuck. It's good to finally meet you."

A small man, tonsured of course, but rather plump especially in comparison to Simon de Poher, came to speak with them.

"The prior," muttered de Poher. "Robert Engayne."

"Nice to meet you too, Father," Tuck said, bowing his head slightly as the little man bustled across to them, round belly shoving a couple of novices out of the way as he passed. "I'm grateful for the hospitality I've been shown since arriving yesterday."

"Please accept my apologies for not being there to greet you," the prior said. His mood seemed a little lighter than his subordinates and Tuck suspected it was because Engayne felt a responsibility not to allow the oppressive atmosphere to affect him. He was the man in charge of Haltemprice, and he was expected to fully believe in God's power to protect them.

"That's quite all right," the friar said, smiling. "Brother De Poher has been a fine host."

"Glad to hear it," nodded the prior, guiding Tuck and the cantor away from the eating monks and into the buttery which was, for the time being, unoccupied. "I've been very busy lately. Haltemprice had some trouble even before we moved into the building, and it's been hard going ever since with the builders and so on. The gardens don't yield as much

25

produce as you'd expect either, and that will have an effect on our income which…" He trailed off and forced a smile. "Never mind all that. Brother de Poher seems to think you might be able to lift the mood in the priory. I'm not sure how, but anything you can do would be most welcome. If I can help at all, let me know." He made the sign of the cross and then, with a quick word of farewell, moved out into the cloister and disappeared from sight.

"A good man," de Poher averred, pointing Tuck towards a space on a nearby bench that had been left vacant for him. The cantor filled a bowl with some porridge and handed it to Tuck along with a single wooden cup of ale.

"Are you not eating?" Tuck practically demanded as he spooned the warm porridge into his mouth. "You'll waste away to nothing, man."

De Poher shook his head, swallowing. "I'm not hungry," he said. Indeed, the very thought of eating seemed anathema to the gaunt cantor, whose skin had taken on an ashen pallor. "You can eat enough for both of us, I'm sure."

Tuck chuckled at that and within moments had indeed emptied his ale, his bowl, and even a second helping of the porridge. He was just wiping his mouth when Prior Engayne stuck his head around the door and gestured to them. They rose immediately and went out into the cloister. Engayne was already walking towards Haltemprice's main entrance, waving for them to follow.

Tuck shared a glance with the cantor. Both had noted the worried expression on the prior's round face and knew something bad must have happened. They hurried after him, curiosity gnawing at Tuck like a dog worrying the marrow from a bone.

The prior went out into the courtyard and the other two followed. A fourth man was there – not a churchman but a farmer Tuck guessed from his clothing, general demeanour, and the pair of sheepdogs that lay on the grass a short distance away, watching everything warily.

"This is Ivo Blaccalf," said the prior, waving his open palm at the man who had a weather-beaten face and hands like hams. "He has the farm up there, on the hill to the west."

Tuck turned and saw a collection of buildings in the distance, a thin column of smoke rising from one of them. No doubt the farmer's wife was cooking up some rustic stew. The thought made Tuck's belly rumble despite it being full already, and he pretended he hadn't heard it as he turned his attention back to Blaccalf.

"Something terrible has happened at the farm . . ." the man was saying in a thick brogue that Tuck had to concentrate on to properly understand. It was amazing how the local dialect could change so much even between communities separated by a handful of miles.

"Tell them," Prior Engayne said, encouraging the farmer who was clearly reticent to say more. "You're with friends here, my good fellow."

"It must have happened during the night," Blaccalf said, jaw clenching and unclenching. He stared at Tuck and there was naked fear in the farmer's gaze. "We heard screaming, and I went out with my dogs and my spear. Thought it were wolves, see, got into my pigs." He trailed off, shaking his head. "It weren't wolves, I'm sure o' that."

"What was it then?" Tuck asked.

"I don't know," the farmer admitted, gaze falling to the ground as he shuffled his feet like a child who doesn't want to talk to his elders. "But whatever it was, it carried off three full grown pigs, and left naught but a bloody stain where the fourth had once stood."

De Poher shuddered and, as he seemed to do so often, swallowed nervously. Tuck was not overly impressed, however, having heard many similar tales from farmers over the years. His friend Will Scaflock kept a farm nowadays and he'd had such things happen too – worse, even. Still, he was careful to keep his tone concerned as he spoke to Blaccalf, understanding how terrible it was for a farmer to lose four valuable hogs.

"Where did the thieves go?" he asked. "Did your dogs follow the trail?"

Blaccalf licked his lips and turned to look back at his distant home on the hillside. "Not at the time," he admitted. Apparently the blight that was afflicting the inhabitants of the priory was also affecting the folk in the surrounding area. "When it was starting to get light we tried, but my dogs lost the trail at the beck. Water must have washed away the scent of whatever took the pigs."

Tuck's brow lifted at the farmer's words. "What do you think took them?"

Blaccalf shrugged and shook his head. "I'd rather not think about it," he muttered. "Anything that can carry off three pigs must be a monster though!"

"God's blood, I'd hate to meet it in the dark there on the moors," de Poher said breathlessly, and even the prior murmured agreement.

"Forgive me," Tuck said, tilting his head in what he hoped was a conciliatory manner. "But I'm not sure why you've brought these tidings here to the priory. What are you hoping the monks can do for you?"

"Pray for us!" Blaccalf returned, the words gushing from him in a wide-eyed torrent. "There's something haunting these hills, and this priory, and only God can save us from it. We've all heard the sounds in the night, seen the devil lights dancing in the darkness when no living man should be abroad."

"We will certainly beg God for his aid," Prior Engayne promised. "Thank you, Ivo, for bringing us this news."

"And thank you," said the farmer. "I'll be sure to leave some alms at the gate on my way out, Father." He wrung his cloth cap in his hands, bowed profusely to the three churchmen, and then strode off, whistling for his dogs to follow.

"Well." The prior looked at Tuck and blew out a long breath. "What d'you make of that, brother?"

"Seems like the strange feeling of dread that hangs over this area is making people jump at shadows."

"Shadows didn't carry off his swine, man," Engayne argued somewhat testily. "Or perhaps they did!"

"What I mean," Tuck said, realizing that he should try to mollify the older man, "is that it sounds to me like someone – people, not monsters – stole his livestock. As happens numerous times up and down the country every day. God forgive me, in my outlaw days I did such things myself by cover of darkness, especially at this time of year when food is scarce."

The prior tutted at that while Simon de Poher looked flabbergasted.

"You may be right," Engayne said, watching the farmer as he headed homewards. "But I fear there's something more to this than simple thievery."

"I'll tell you what, Father," Tuck said. "I'll ride out myself and see if I can find some trace of the missing pigs."

Engayne seemed surprised at the offer. "Ride out? Alone? There?" He gestured towards the hills which, in the dim morning light did look rather sinister.

Tuck nodded firmly. "Why not? I'm a warrior as well as a man of God."

"But…alone?"

The friar pulled back his cloak to reveal the cudgel tucked into his rope belt. "I'll be fine, Father. This has kept me safe more than once over the years. And this." He let go of the cloak and reached up to touch the simple wooden cross on a leather thong around his neck. "Earthly, or unearthly, whatever stalks these lands will find me a tough opponent to best."

"That may be," Prior Engayne smiled. "But you don't know the area so you will take Brother de Poher with you as a guide. Good luck, gentlemen!"

SIX

The wind had died down by the time Tuck and Simon de Poher rode through Haltemprice Priory's gates towards the distant farm in the west. In truth, the friar was glad to leave behind the stifling stone walls for a time, even if it did mean he would be exposed to the elements and whatever else might haunt the surrounding moors.

There were times when the friar carried a sword – he could wield one with just as much skill as his trusty cudgel – but he had not brought it to the priory with him. Instead, he had his quarterstaff for extra protection but he really did not think he would need it and it was safely stowed, upright, on his horse's saddle. Brother de Poher carried a knife although Tuck didn't expect the monk to be much use if it came to a fight.

The sun did not break through the clouds that seemed to swirl over Haltemprice eternally but it was warmer than the previous day and the lack of howling wind made the atmosphere less oppressive, if not exactly pleasant.

Tuck's eyes scanned the fields about him as they made their way to the farm. The land here was mostly uninhabited, with just the odd, solitary house or tiny settlement visible, and the terrain rose higher the further west one went. The grain that had grown during the summer months had been harvested and all around was a faded green or brown with barely even a tree to brighten the scene. It was, all things considered, rather a dull looking place and the friar wondered if it was a crushing sense of boredom that was affecting the monks rather than any malevolent presence.

There was no sign of Ivo Blaccalf on the track to the farm and Tuck guessed he'd hurried home so he could be about his usual business. The life of a farmer was a hard one, up at the crack of dawn and busy labouring until late into the evening. The friar did not envy Blaccalf and, although he suspected the man was more superstitious than was warranted, he felt pity for the loss of his expensive pigs and truly hoped to locate them. Alive, if possible…

As they neared Blaccalf's steading Tuck noticed shallow ruts in the earth, leading south. He dismounted and examined them, wondering if this might be the method used to carry off the pigs. He could picture the cart that had made the tracks – two-wheeled, and small enough to be pulled by a single horse or even a man.

"Look," he said to de Poher, pointing to the beck. "These cart tracks lead down there. That must be where the farmer's dogs lost the scent. Let's go and take a look."

They rode down the hill together and, sure enough, the cart's tracks did not come out of the water on the opposite bank from where they went in, but Tuck guided his palfrey along the grass for a few paces, eyes fixed downwards. Just as he was beginning to think he should try in the other direction the tracks reappeared, heading west again – Blaccalf had not put much effort into following the tracks, but the friar could hardly blame him. Perhaps Tuck should give up too at this point, for who knew what horrors lay at the end of the trail?

The ground was rising once more and Tuck pictured a man, maybe even more than one, dragging the cart uphill in the gloom, buffeted by the gusting wind and cursing at the effort. Clearly, they had thought it worth it.

Tuck rode faster now for the cart's path clearly followed a well-worn if narrow, winding road. As he was carried higher towards the top of a low hill the sense of foreboding returned and Tuck actually reached down and took his quarterstaff out from where it was buckled to the horse's saddle.

"Is something wrong?" de Poher called from behind him.

"No, don't worry, Simon," Tuck shouted, smiling over his shoulder reassuringly. "I just like to be prepared for anything, and who knows what we might find at the top of this hill?"

The air had grown very cold and there was a hint of moisture which made the friar's grey robe clammy and uncomfortable. The palfrey also sensed the change in their surroundings, growing restless and skittish as it drew closer to the summit.

When the road brought them to the top of the hill Tuck sucked a breath through his teeth and, glancing around to make sure there were no obvious threats nearby, jumped down from the saddle. He pegged the horse to the ground so it would not run off in a panic, which seemed a distinct possibility for they had found the missing pigs.

"Oh, God save us," Brother de Poher gasped, practically falling off the back of his horse and wringing his hands with so much force that Tuck feared he might hurt himself. "What's happened to them? Christ in Heaven, do I even want to know?"

The pigs were clearly dead, and the hairy, long-legged animals had been laid it out in what looked to Tuck like some bizarre ritualistic fashion. The three bodies were on their sides in the shape of a rough, expansive triangle. Their bellies had been slit open and the entrails torn out then laid on the ground in the shape of some strange symbol. The friar did not know what they meant, but he had seen such symbols before, in the occult books owned by delvers into hidden mysteries like Edward Magnus. In the centre of it all was a large stone with the remnants of something that had been burned, most likely the hearts of the dead beasts – a final touch to the hellish, hilltop ceremony.

It was not just the sight of the pigs that shocked the friar though, it was also the smell. Over the usual scent of butchered and burned meat there was something even more disturbing. He walked slowly around the dreadful scene, wondering where he'd smelled that odour before. It was sweet and cloying and fusty, and Tuck remembered now that same malodorous stench in Edward Magnus's chamber beneath Haltemprice Priory.

What caused it? Tuck forced himself to bend down beside the nearest cadaver and even to nudge the thing to one side. Beneath it there was a blue-grey powder of some sort which the friar immediately recognised as being the source of the smell. He was loath to touch it but to his eyes it looked much like salt, although of coarser grain and of a darker, greyer hue.

Just what the hell was going on here? Had the cellarer, Edward Magnus, left alone from Haltemprice Priory with a cart, carrying off three adult pigs and sacrificing them to some insane devil on this hilltop in the dead of night? The idea seemed incredible, but someone had done this, whether it was Magnus or not.

"What is the purpose of all this?" de Poher asked, clearly terrified by the hideous scene. He dashed tears from his eyes. "I can see it's some kind of ritual, but what was it supposed to achieve?"

Tuck shook his head but had no reply for his old friend. He held his pectoral cross, drawing strength from the smooth, familiar wood, and clasped his hands, reciting the Pater Noster with Brother de Poher before asking God to cleanse the hilltop of its evil taint. Then he used his staff to destroy the blasphemous symbols formed by the offal and, feeling decidedly nauseous, mounted his horse.

"Come on, Simon," the friar murmured, patting the nervous palfrey's neck as they began the descent back to Haltemprice. "Let's get away from this evil place and report what we've found to the farmer and Prior Engayne."

And then, he thought grimly to himself, I'll need to have another word with Edward Magnus and find out where he was last night.

SEVEN

The prior was stunned by the news of Tuck and de Poher's gruesome discovery on the nearby hilltop when they returned to Haltemprice. The three men spent some time in the unoccupied refectory discussing what to do about the carcasses left by the hateful ritual, wondering whether to burn, bury, or simply leave them for fear of being somehow tainted themselves by transference of dark, residual energy. In the end, Prior Engayne decided that to leave the blasphemous scene as it was would be wrong.

"I'll go myself to meet the farmer, Blaccalf," he said, closing his eyes and massaging them tiredly. "And we shall remove the pigs to be buried in unconsecrated ground."

"I'd suggest beheading them," Tuck said. "And staking them to the ground before you fill in the graves."

The prior gawped at him. "They're just pigs, brother," he said, incredulous.

Tuck shrugged. "Better safe than sorry," he said. "You don't want dead, demon pigs running around the moors. I've heard tales—"

"Yes, yes," Engayne broke in, waving his hand to silence Tuck as de Poher moaned in terror. "We've all heard tales. You're right. I'll have the farmer bring some wire and a mallet to stake the bodies down."

"It's not a pretty sight," Tuck warned him.

"No, I'm sure it's not. And I have no experience in such matters as this. Black magic…" He trailed off, visibly steeling himself for the task ahead. "I'll take the cellarer with me," he said. "He knows more about demonology and the occult than anyone in Haltemprice."

Tuck stared at him. Rather than assuming Edward Magnus had been involved in the ritual slaughter, the prior was going to turn to the man for advice? Well, if the prior and Simon de Poher both trusted the man, perhaps Tuck should too. He'd only met the cellarer once after all, and that for just a few moments of male posturing in which Tuck may have been as bad as Magnus.

"I must prepare for the short journey," Prior Engayne was saying, bringing Tuck back to the present. "Bible, candles, holy water. There's much to pack, I imagine, and I don't want to get all the way up that hillside only to realise I've forgotten something."

Tuck bowed and headed for the door. "I'll go down and speak with Edward Magnus if you wish. Tell him what's happened and that you wish him to accompany you to bless the hilltop and bury the butchered carcasses."

The prior glanced up at him and smiled, the deep lines on his face easing momentarily. "That would be most helpful, Brother Tuck, thank you."

"My pleasure," replied the friar. "Will you come with me?" he asked de Poher.

"I'm afraid not," the monk replied, a far-away look on his face as though he was finding it hard to forget what he'd seen that morning. "I have duties to attend to and I'm already behind."

Tuck patted him gently on the arm and left the room, heading out along the cloister to the steps that led down to the undercroft. Now he had a reason to visit the cellarer's subterranean domain, and he meant to make the most of it. Maybe he had unfairly judged Edward Magnus, and maybe he should trust the judgement of the monks who knew the goatish cellarer better, but Tuck was adept at reading men. He'd had a lot of practice at it, and something about Magnus rubbed the friar the wrong way.

It would be dark in the undercroft obviously, so Tuck did as they'd done yesterday and quickly visited the library to borrow a candle. Two elderly monks were in the room reading, and they glanced irritably at him as he quickly made a flame with his flint, steel and dried nettle tinder and brought the candle to life.

As he moved silently down the steps into the gloomy undercroft Tuck felt a familiar, heavy sensation in the pit of his stomach: fear, and excitement. Aye, strange things were happening in Haltemprice Priory, and there was a distinct sense of impending danger surrounding the place, but Friar Tuck was glad he'd been summoned there by Simon de Poher.

He meant to get to the bottom of this mystery, and something was telling him he'd find all the answers he needed there in that malodorous cellar.

EIGHT

The familiar, fusty smell assailed Tuck's nostrils almost as soon as he started the descent into Edward Magnus's domain. He slowed, trying to figure out what exactly the scent consisted of. It was not anything he recognised from living either in a house of God or as an outlaw in the greenwood. It didn't seem natural to the friar and perhaps that was what made him so on edge. The stench was heady and otherworldly and, dare he say it, even eldritch in nature – whatever it came from was not anything wholesome, that much was certain. It pervaded the whole undercroft it seemed, and Tuck took his time as he walked along the main passageway, sticking his head into the open chambers that branched off. Most of them looked to be used for storage, with old furniture, barrels of ale, and other everyday items revealed by his guttering candle. Ahead, in the chamber the cellarer used as his private study, no light shone and Tuck felt the excitement grow within him again.

He had the place to himself, at least for a short time.

Hurrying, his steps rang overly loud as he went into the room and found another candle which he also lit before setting his original in a sconce in the wall. He looked around and saw the bookcase, noting that it was now stocked with all the occult volumes that had previously been stored upstairs in the library. They had been moved down here for some reason, but Tuck only wanted to look through one of them at this moment: the grimoire Edward Magnus had been reading the day before.

Glancing over his shoulder at the passageway to make sure he was alone, Tuck went to the tome and looked at it, running his hands across the leather binding. With a start, he realised it might not actually be leather after all, but human skin. Such abominations were uncommon, he knew, but did exist.

Still, the chances of this particular volume being so bound were tiny, and he feared he was allowing his imagination to run away with him. Lifting it, he examined the title, *Necronomicon*, and wondered what it meant. It was obviously a very valuable tome and, when he held it flat it fell open of its own accord, just as it had done when Tuck watched Magnus with it.

Taking a deep breath through his nose to steady himself, the friar placed the heavy book down on the desk and gazed at it. There was writing, but, as with the title, Tuck did not recognise the language. There was also a drawing of what looked like a pile of everyday salt or dust captioned, 'Salz des Lebens'.

"God's bones," Tuck breathed, staring at the pages in bemusement. "What does this all mean? Salt? Is he cooking a meal? Was that what the pigs' hearts were for?"

The air within the cellar was close and the fusty smell was making the friar light headed but, just as he was reaching out to pull the nearest chair over to him a voice said, "What the devil are you doing in here?"

Tuck spun around, hand falling instinctively to his hidden cudgel, but he was dizzier than he realised and found his legs giving way.

Edward Magnus stood before him, eyes blazing, but the cellarer stretched out his arms and grabbed hold of the friar, holding him up and guiding him to the chair.

Tuck's head swam and he wondered how Magnus had managed to sneak up on him. The man must be able to move like a cat! He also must be much stronger than his lean frame suggested, for the friar was tall and heavily built yet Magnus had held him up seemingly with little effort.

"Are you well?" The words were sympathetic, but the tone they were spoken in was belligerent and Tuck sat in silence for a long moment, trying to regain his equilibrium.

"I came over a little light headed," he admitted at last.

"The air in this chamber can do that to a person," Magnus told him. "Certain…ingredients and components from my studies have left behind a somewhat noxious atmosphere. It's fine once you're used to it, as I am, but for one such as you? Well, you see the effects it can have."

"I'm feeling a little better now," Tuck lied, still amazed by the cellarer's strength.

"You should leave," Magnus nodded, turning to wave a hand towards the passageway. "But first, why are you down here at all? The monks know not to come into my study uninvited. I would have expected better manners than this from a visitor."

"The prior sent me," Tuck said, looking up and meeting the angry gaze of the cellarer. "There's been a terrible crime committed. The ritual sacrifice of three stolen pigs, up on a hilltop to the west." He watched Magnus's face for some reaction but there was nothing.

"Has there now?"

"Aye," Tuck said. "Prior Engayne is going to bury the carcasses and bless the hilltop. He wants you to go with him as you are, apparently, an authority on this kind of thing."

Now the cellarer's mouth did twitch in the ghost of a proud smile. "Compared to the fools in this priory I am certainly an expert on many things."

"Well, that's why I came down here."

"I see," Magnus replied, never taking his eyes from him as he reached down and closed the *Necronomicon* before placing it into an empty space on one of the shelves. "And you just thought you would read my books while you were here, eh?"

Tuck smiled broadly. "Like you, Edward, I'm an avid reader, and my curiosity got the better of me. I could not resist taking a little peek."

Magnus grunted, his slightly curled lip suggesting he did not believe a word of Tuck's explanation.

"Are you fit to stand, brother?" the cellarer demanded coldly. "Yes? Then be off with you. I must gather some things for the ritual with Prior Engayne. Tell him I will be ready to leave shortly. And, Brother Tuck?"

"Yes?"

"Do not come down here again. If you do, you will suffer more than a little dizziness."

Anger flared within Tuck then. He was not used to being spoken to in such a dismissive, threatening tone and part of him wanted to berate the cellarer for his rudeness. To teach the fool some manners.

And then he remembered that he had, indeed, entered Magnus's little domain uninvited and taken it upon himself to touch the man's valuable book. True, it hardly warranted the cellarer's scolding but there was no point in responding with aggression of his own. He was still feeling queasy and a brawl between the two of them would hardly be seemly. Perhaps that was what Edward Magnus wanted – Tuck would surely be sent home to Wakefield if a fight was to break out.

"Where were you last night?" the friar suddenly demanded, unwilling to leave without casting one last barb at the cellarer.

"I was in my cell, sleeping," Magnus replied with a mocking smile, as if he knew no one could prove otherwise. "Now get out."

"I'll tell Prior Engayne that you will meet him shortly," the friar said in as level a tone as he could manage and then he turned and headed slowly for the passageway, not even remembering to take his candle.

As he passed the storage rooms with their black, gaping doorways Tuck realised men were standing within them, watching him pass. He felt the hairs on his neck rise but forced himself to move on without looking back. The light from Magnus's chamber was just enough for him to make out the faces and dress of those silent watchers – they were not monks, but burly servants. Obviously lackeys of Edward Magnus.

Tuck made his way safely up the stairs and, when he was once more alone in the cloisters breathing fresh, clean air, he stopped to rest for a moment, relieved not to have been attacked.

Whatever the cellarer and his servants were doing in the undercroft was not the work of any good Christian, Tuck was certain of that. "Salz des Lebens," he murmured to himself, committing the foreign phrase to his memory. He could not understand what it meant, but he would surely find someone within Haltemprice Priory who did, and perhaps then Tuck would have some clue as to Edward Magnus's sinister purpose.

But first, Tuck must send a message to Wakefield.

This mystery was too much for one man to safely investigate – he needed help, and he knew exactly whom to turn to.

NINE

"God's bollocks, I've seen more inspiring views in a latrine." Will Scaflock, more widely known as Scarlet, stared out at the almost featureless landscape around Haltemprice Priory and heaved a sigh. "And it's bloody cold too."

Even the usually jovial John Little barely mustered a smile at his friend's outburst as they rode through the priory gates and gazed around at the new buildings.

"Boy!" Scarlet's roar filled the courtyard and the young stablehand looked up from his fingernails. He'd been cleaning the dirt out from under them with a little knife and his sullen expression did not impress either of the riders.

"Get your arse over here and deal with our horses," John called, smiling to offset the harshness of his words.

The boy sidled over to them as they lifted their packs from their horses and an older man came out of the stables to join them.

"Is this how you greet all your visitors?" Will asked as the youth took the reins and led his horse to a stall.

"Begging your pardon, sir. I didn't notice you."

"Didn't notice us?" John laughed. Now that he was standing on the ground his immense size was clear. Standing over six and half feet tall, the older stablehand gazed up at him although there was a hard, almost challenging edge to his tone as he offered a half-hearted apology.

"Sorry, sirs. We'll make sure your mounts are well cared for. Forgive the boy, he's moon-touched."

The venomous glance the lad threw over his shoulder suggested that was not true, but Will and John were bored with the conversation now. When they'd been outlaws people had often treated them disrespectfully and they'd grown used to it. It did not happen so often nowadays, but they had more important things to think about than a couple of rude servants.

From somewhere deep inside the priory the monks' deep voices rose and fell in plainsong – the rhythmic, chanted prayers of the brothers' daily devotions that could bring some Christians, like St Augustine, to tears.

"Is someone going to come and meet us then?" John demanded, scanning the closed windows and doors of the priory. He, at least, was not moved by the Gregorian chant of the monks.

Before the sullen stablehand could reply the main entrance was flung open and the familiar round face of Friar Tuck appeared. "There you are at last!" he said. "What took you so long?"

John and Scarlet shared a glance as they walked towards their friend.

"Long? We came as soon as we got your message, and were only on the road two days."

Tuck nodded, beaming as they reached him and they gripped forearms. "It felt like you took forever to get here. This priory…" He held up his palms and looked around. "You lose track of the days after a while with all the routine, and the singing. It's a very strange place."

"Aye, we noticed," Scarlet said. "Felt like someone, or something, was watching us the closer we came. And that mist – it's midday and still hasn't lifted. Seeps into the very bones!"

"I know," Tuck murmured. "I spent my time waiting for your arrival by reading in the library and taking walks. The mist rarely seems to lift, and when it does the wind takes its place."

"Why have you brought us here, Tuck?" John asked as the main door was closed. "Your message wasn't very clear."

"I didn't want to write down my suspicions in case someone intercepted the messenger," the friar told them in a low voice as he led them around the cloister to the refectory. "But I'm glad you've come, and I'll explain everything to you in a bit. First, you'll be hungry and thirsty so follow me and we'll see about finding some sustenance."

The travellers visibly brightened at that and soon they were seated in the refectory enjoying a meal of fish with peas and buttered bread.

"At least those servants aren't as belligerent as the two arseholes in the stables," Scarlet murmured, pointing his spoon at the back of the middle-aged man who'd brought them their food.

"He didn't exactly look cheery either," John pointed out, washing down a mouthful of food with freshly brewed, dark ale.

"There seems to be two kinds of monk and layperson here in the priory," Tuck told them, leaning in so he wouldn't be overheard. "There's a handful, like the stablehands, who give the impression they might start a fight with you given any minor provocation, and then there's the rest who just appear browbeaten and depressed most of the time."

"Start a fight?" Will gave a wry chuckle. "With us three? Let 'em try ."

John smiled at him through his grizzled beard and fed some more fish into his mouth.

"I'd rather avoid any fighting if possible," Tuck said, still keeping his voice low and even looking over his shoulder at the door to the cloister. "Although there's two or three of the ugly bastards I'll be glad to teach some manners if they get in my way."

John downed the last of his ale and smacked his lips loudly before running his sleeve across his mouth. "That was good," he said approvingly. "But I'm dying to know what the hell is going on here, Tuck so, if we're all done here, can you please tell us?"

Will muttered agreement and the friar nodded, standing and offering his thanks to the servant who came to clear the table. "Follow me then, lads," he said to his friends. "We'll take a walk in the gardens and I'll tell you all about it."

* * *

The three men strolled through the gardens of Haltemprice Priory but one of the servants that Tuck had noticed in the undercroft a few days earlier was lurking about again. The man was broad and muscular with a scar on his cheek and the kind of nose that belonged to a lifelong pugilist. He did not look like the kind of servant houses of God usually employed to work in the gardens – he looked like a soldier.

Tuck had spotted the fellow and it seemed clear he was attempting to eavesdrop although with all the subtlety of a braying calf. So, the friar led his friends out of the priory grounds and across the moors to the west, not walking fast or straying too far, but making it utterly impossible for their shadow to follow without making it obvious.

"What's his problem?" Will demanded when they were some distance away from the garden. He'd not hidden his irritation at the servant and might well have started a brawl if they'd hung around the priory much longer.

"Ignore him for now," Tuck said. "And let me explain everything that's been going on here."

He filled them in on what Simon de Poher had told him in his original letter, and what he'd encountered in the time he'd spent in the priory since he'd arrived. Not only had he been rudely spoken to by Edward Magnus and made to leave the cellar under an unspoken but implicit threat of violence, but Tuck's rest had been disturbed too.

"I've had terrible dreams every night I've been here," the friar told his companions.

"What about?"

"I don't know, John. That's the thing, I can never recall them, even straight after waking up." He shook his head and rubbed his smooth chin in consternation. "They're terrifying, I know that but…" His voice faded and he glanced up at the sky as a gust of wind whipped at his cloak. "The wind. Always that damned wind."

"Bad dreams, bad smells, nasty people, and some ritually sacrificed pigs." Will shrugged his wide shoulders and fingered the pommel of his sword contemplatively. "I still don't really see why you needed us here."

Tuck cocked his head and nodded. "Indeed, that does not sound like much cause for concern," he admitted. "But I'm sure those servants of Magnus are actively seeking to do me harm. Someone's been trying the door to my cell at night."

"What?" John was outraged. Although the three men enjoyed banter and often insulted one another they were firm friends, with bonds of loyalty that had been forged in their white-hot days as hunted outlaws.

"It's true," the friar said grimly. "But I've been propping my chair against the door since I arrived. The sinister atmosphere had me on edge and, since the cell doors don't have a proper lock, I used the chair. Just as well, for I'm quite a heavy sleeper."

"Oh, we know," Scarlet snorted, and he and John laughed. "Your snoring has kept us, and half the animals in the forest, awake many times over the years."

"Aye, well," Tuck returned indignantly, "I'm not so heavy a sleeper that the sound of the door rattling against my chair won't wake me. Unfortunately, by the time I'd grabbed my cudgel and thrown the door open whoever was trying to get in had fled. You can see why I fear for my own safety though, eh?"

"Why not just ride home to Wakefield?" John asked, drawing his hood up around his neck as the wind continued to pick up, howling across the moors and through the few trees that dotted the dreary landscape.

"Because there is a real mystery here," Tuck said, eyes dancing. "I must get to the bottom of it. Leaving is simply out of the question and, now that I have you two to protect me, I can stop worrying about being murdered in my bed."

The three men sat on a fallen tree and pondered Tuck's words.

"What are we going to do then?" John asked after a long moment.

"Do?" Scarlet asked incredulously. "We're going to deal with those servants. We'll show the bastards what happens to anyone who threatens one of our friends. And then we'll get a hold of the cellarer, what's his name? Edward Magnus, and beat the truth out of him." He laughed nastily. "It'll be just like the old days."

"I like it," John said, grinning and tapping his fingers on the great quarterstaff that was even taller than him.

"Have you two gone insane?" Tuck demanded, standing up, hands on his hips as he glared at them as if they were misbehaving children. "In the good old days we were wolf's heads, and we didn't care about the law. Now? You're a respectable farmer, Will!"

"Respectable," John sniggered, earning a thump from Scarlet.

"And you, John Little? You're a bailiff, by God! We can't just go around assaulting high-ranking members of the clergy."

"But it's so much fun," Scarlet protested.

"Maybe if they deserve it," Tuck admitted, smiling himself now. "But we have to prove Edward Magnus and his henchmen are up to something illegal first."

"And then we can beat the shit out of them?" John asked.

"I'll throw the first punch myself," the friar vowed. "That smug cellarer has it coming. But" – he held up a hand and stood, the gusting wind whipping the hem of his heavy cloak – "first we gather evidence. We don't even know what exactly he's up to, or why."

"Fair enough," John said, getting up and stretching. "Let's get on with it then. I don't want to hang around these bleak lands for any longer than absolutely necessary."

TEN

Since Will and John were laymen rather than churchmen they were not given cells in the dormitory, or even in the main priory building. Instead, they were allocated quarters in the guesthouse which was located near to the stables. With Tuck no longer feeling safe sleeping in the cell he'd been given, he also moved his things to the guesthouse. It would be truly lavish accommodation when finished, but this was one of the areas the builders had not quite completed so, although the roof was in place and the doors and windows locked, there were not many furnishings. Still, the men had slept in far worse places over the years and settled in quite happily.

That first night was spent with Tuck filling in even more detail on what he knew about Haltemprice Priory and its cellarer, Edward Magnus.

"What about your friend?" Will asked him.

"Simon de Poher," Tuck said. "I haven't seen him much over the past couple of days. I suspect Brother Magnus has had a word with him, warned him to stop meddling in things that don't concern him."

"Really?" John asked doubtfully. "Could it be possible your friend has something to do with all the trouble, and has backed away from you now that he sees we're serious about discovering the truth?"

"Simon?" Tuck laughed heartily at the bailiff's suggestion. "If you'd met him, you wouldn't even suggest that. He's as quiet and timid as a mouse.

There's no way he'd be involved in something like this."

"He's never done anything he shouldn't have in the past?" Will asked. "I remember when I was a monk there were a few brothers who acted like butter wouldn't melt in their mouths but they were secretly getting up to all sorts of things. Drinking, fighting, fu—"

"Simon isn't doing any of that," Tuck retorted, cutting Scarlet off mid-sentence. He cast his mind back over the years though, frowning as he remembered one incident. "There was a suggestion that Simon had pushed a fellow monk down some stairs, but that was a long time ago and I don't think anything came of it."

"What?" John demanded, laughing incredulously.

"The other fellow had been bullying Simon mercilessly," Tuck told them, trying his best to recall the details. "I didn't see any of it, but witnesses claimed it had been no accident when the other monk fell and broke his legs."

"That paints a different picture of Brother de Poher," Will noted. "Maybe he's not the timid mouse you think he is."

"He denied pushing the bully," Tuck argued. "And, like I say, nothing came of it. Simon doesn't have it in him to be violent. He had nothing to do with that incident, and he has nothing to do with what's happening here. Why would he invite me here if he was involved?"

The wind had picked up throughout the day and it whistled now through gaps in the window frames and under the door. Normally Tuck would have felt cosy and secure on a night like this, safely locked away indoors, but the sense of approaching doom that haunted Haltemprice did not allow for such pleasant feelings. It almost felt to Tuck as if he was simply waiting for something to come and find them. Something deeply sinister and absolutely unstoppable.

"What's our next move then?" Will asked.

"I don't know," Tuck admitted, staring into the small fire that burned in the hearth beside him. They had purposely kept it low because of the wind, fearful some sudden gust might blow hot embers into the room and set the whole place alight.

"What if someone were to go out in the dark just now?" John asked.

"Eh?" Tuck asked, confused. "Who would go out in this weather? At night? The monks should all be abed by this time."

"Well, they're not," John told him, and Tuck only realised now that his giant friend was looking out of the glazed window, peering into the courtyard. "Someone with a tonsure is creeping about out there, I can see the moonlight reflected on his head. He's walking towards the gate and…" He paused, leaning back a little so he wouldn't be as visible at the window. "There are more men following the first one. Two of them. Not monks."

"Servants," Will breathed, joining Little John at the glass and squinting into the benighted courtyard. "But look. They're carrying something on their backs. Maybe weapons."

"What the devil are they up to?" Tuck murmured. He was on his feet and pulling on his heavy cloak, checking his cudgel was in position before lifting his quarterstaff. They had a choice – go after whoever was creeping about in the night, or, assuming it was Edward Magnus, take the chance to head down to the undercroft once again and search it more thoroughly in his absence. "Come on," he said, realising the undercroft would probably be locked up tight anyway. "We'll follow them."

He did not need to remind John and Scarlet to bring their weapons. Will had his sword and a longbow with a dozen arrows, while John carried sword and quarterstaff. It would be a brave enemy who challenged the three former outlaws, for their martial skills were legendary.

They extinguished the candles and left the fire to burn itself out as they slipped into the darkness and moved soundlessly across the courtyard towards the gates.

"Does no one guard these?" Will asked as they passed through unchallenged. "Or even lock the bloody things in the evening?"

Tuck shrugged although it went unseen in the darkness. "I don't know. I'm sure they've been closed at times since I've been here, although I don't remember ever seeing anyone actually guarding them."

"Haltemprice is full of valuable items a thief would gladly walk off with," John groused as they followed the three shadowy figures in the distance. "What's the point in sturdy gates if they lie open all night, inviting anyone to walk in?"

"Or out," Scarlet added, hissing as one of the far-off men paused as if turning to look back at them. "Hide!"

There was a bramble bush beside them and all three threw themselves into it, cursing as the thorns tore at their skin and clothing.

"God's cock, this is ridiculous," Scarlet hissed. "Why don't we just catch up with the bastards and force them to tell us what they're up to?"

"Don't be daft," Tuck chided. "And watch your language, Will Scaflock, especially so close to a priory."

"Come on, they never spotted us." John was already on his feet again and moving like a massive wraith across the moonlit moor.

They followed their quarry for quite some time until, at last, Tuck realised his suspicions about their destination had proved correct. "This is the way to Ivo Blaccalf's farm," he said.

"Then those three up ahead are looking for more animals to sacrifice," John guessed. "The pigs weren't enough for whatever the ritual was supposed to achieve, so they're going to do it all again."

"With what?" Will wondered. "What could be more potent than pigs? Sheep? Chickens?"

"I don't think so," Tuck said, pausing to catch his breath and to let the men ahead move away a little. "They have nothing to carry animals in. No cart."

"Two of them have long poles strapped to their backs," John said, pointing up at the black figures on the skyline. "See them? They could lash a carcass to those and share the load."

They fell silent again as they hurried onwards, Tuck assuring them the farm was not far away now.

By the time they reached the wooden building that Blaccalf called his home all was quiet, other than the whistling wind.

"Where the hell did they go?" Scarlet growled, eyes scanning the gloom but detecting no sight or sound of the mysterious travellers from the priory.

"I don't know," Tuck admitted. "Perhaps we should rouse the farmer. He can bring his dogs and help us search the area."

Their chattering had been low but apparently not quiet enough for a furious barking came to them then from the nearby farmhouse and the shutters on one of the windows was thrown open, revealing a pale, frightened face lit by a lantern. "Who's that out there?" Blaccalf bellowed. "Speak, or I'll let the dogs out!"

"It's Friar Tuck! We met earlier at the priory."

"What in God's name are you doing out there in the dark?" the farmer asked, tone still tense and threatening.

"We saw three men walking towards your farm," Tuck called back. "But we've lost sight of them. Perhaps you should come out and bring your dogs to help us find them, for they're surely up to no good."

That was enough to bring Blaccalf outdoors. He came with two skittish sheepdogs on lengths of rope, whining and snarling and snapping at Tuck and his companions. "Where are the whoresons?" the farmer cried, his lantern making sinister shadows dance around the yard. "I'll not stand here and let them steal any more of my livestock."

"Let's take a look around then," Tuck suggested. "Maybe you should let the dogs search?"

"Who's that?" Blaccalf asked, a note of fear entering his voice as he finally noticed just how large Tuck's friends were.

"Little John and Will Scaflock," the friar replied. "They're with me. Come, we have no time to lose, Blaccalf. All this noise will have alerted the men that were lurking about here."

The farmer nodded and knelt to talk with his dogs, giving them some unintelligible commands in his thick Yorkshire brogue before letting them off their ropes. Rather than running to attack the former outlaws the hounds raced off into the darkness.

"Those two can smell a predator from a mile away," Blaccalf said proudly, watching as the dogs disappeared. "Listen for the sounds of screaming." He laughed nastily and they all stood straining their ears for some sign that the intruders had been tracked down.

There was nothing other than the snuffling and scrabbling paws of the sheepdogs. No shouts of pain, no screams, no pleas for the farmer to call off the hounds, nothing.

"There's no one around now," Blaccalf said, relief vying with suspicion on his face as he turned his gaze once more on his three visitors. "If there ever was."

"We trailed them here," John replied levelly. "Maybe you should check your animals, make sure they're all accounted for."

The farmer did not reply for a long moment as his dogs continued to snuffle and run around in the darkness nearby, but then one of them must have picked up a scent for they suddenly came back towards the house but did not stop, running right past Blaccalf towards a low building to the north.

All four men followed the dog, knowing it had discovered something.

"What's that building?" Scarlet asked.

"Stables," the farmer replied tightly. He'd drawn out a knife, long blade glinting menacingly in the lantern light, and he brandished it before him as they came to the wooden building. Blaccalf could tell where he was even in the gloom and he moved along the locked stalls, checking them. Three times he let out a furious oath until he eventually turned to Tuck and said, "Some of my horses are gone."

"Horses?" John asked. "Would they take horses for a ritual sacrifice?"

Blaccalf gave a strangled cry at the suggestion. Losing valuable horses so soon after his pigs would be a terrible financial blow to the farmer.

"Would they, Tuck?" Will asked, biting his lip. For all his vicious temper towards humans he loved animals and the idea of horses being ritualistically murdered greatly disturbed him.

The friar swallowed and licked his lips, staring at the empty stalls with a terrible sense of dread in his guts. "It wouldn't be the first time someone has done something like that," he admitted quietly. "These people are evil — they'll use the blood of anything they can to appease their dark masters and the bigger the sacrifice the better."

"You have to stop them!" Blaccalf cried, looking at the three friends with a pleading expression on his ruddy face.

"How?" Will asked, taking a deep breath and looking up at the stable roof as he leaned back against the wall. "Even your dogs won't be able to track three riders across the moors in the dark. By the time we catch up to them it'll be morning and whatever they have planned will be finished."

"Who are they?" the farmer demanded, fists balled, tears of rage filling his eyes.

Little John opened his mouth but Tuck reached out and squeezed his arm, silencing him. They could not accuse Edward Magnus – they hadn't seen the three shadowy figures clearly enough to positively identify any of them. Blaming the cellarer for heinous, blasphemous crimes would not go well if they did not have proof to back up the accusations. And Magnus would undoubtedly have servants willing to give him an alibi for this night's work.

"We don't know," Tuck said, meeting the farmer's anguished gaze. "But we are going to find out, Ivo, I promise you. And when we do, the bastards will swing for their crimes."

"What now?" John asked, deflated from this disappointing end to the chase.

"We go back to the priory," Tuck said. "And see what the morning brings."

There was nothing else for it. They left the farmer in a pool of lantern light, tears of rage glistening in his eyes, and trudged back across the windswept moors to the guest house at Haltemprice Priory. Will and John would have gone hunting right then for Edward Magnus, either in his bed or in his lair in the undercroft, but Tuck rejected the plan. As he reiterated, they had no proof Magnus was one of the three men creeping about on the hill and causing such a fuss in the middle of the night would not endear them to the monks or Prior Engayne.

They would simply need to catch as much sleep as they could, and pray to God that the three stolen horses turned up safe and well the next day.

As Tuck lay on his sleeping pallet with John's soft snores filling the building he had a terrible premonition that Blaccalf would never see his animals alive again and, as sleep slowly drew its black veil over him the now familiar nightmares came to him.

ELEVEN

Regardless of his tortured dreams, Tuck's prediction was proved wrong. The horses were found the next day, safely back in one of Ivo Blaccalf's fields. It seemed they had been set loose once the thieves had completed their purpose, whatever it was, and the clever animals had made their way back home.

"Well this is good news indeed," said Tuck, rubbing his face and trying to clear the lingering taint of his nightmares. As ever, he could not remember them other than vague images and impressions of ancient evil lurking around Haltemprice; ancient evil that meant to make an end to everyone in the priory and the surrounding lands.

"Good news, aye," John agreed. He'd had a good sleep, undisturbed by nightmares or anxieties over amorphous threats to his life and sanity. John was a Christian, as they all were, but he was not as superstitious as Tuck – he'd seen too many things in recent years that proved, to his satisfaction at least, that humanity posed far more danger to him than demons or ghouls.

"The farmer was here at the very crack of dawn to let us know," Will Scarlet said. "I was across in the refectory looking for breakfast."

"Did you find it?" Tuck asked, splashing his face with water and doing his best to wash away the fog that lingered over his mind.

"Aye," Scarlet said, throwing a chunk of bread to the friar who caught it nimbly and bit into it happily.

"I'd forgotten what it was like to eat a meal in a house of God. All the brothers sitting there eating in silence."

"Silence?" John demanded, amazed.

"Aye," Scarlet confirmed. "Meals are a time for contemplation, not making jokes and talking nonsense to one another."

"So," John said with a sardonic laugh. "Meal times are just like every other time in a priory."

"I suppose so," Scarlet said, smiling himself. "It's not the most exciting life, I'll grant you that."

"Did the farmer have anything else to say about the horses?" Tuck asked. "Any clue as to who might have taken them, or why?"

Scarlet shook his head and sat down on a stool to wait for his companions to get ready for the morning ahead. "Nah, nothing like that. He just wanted to let us know the horses had returned and hadn't been sacrificed as we'd all feared."

"Well, this is a very pleasant way to start the day," Tuck said, finishing his bread and washing his mouth and teeth with some fresh water that Scarlet had also brought from the refectory. "I had a terrible feeling that those three men we trailed were going to commit some hideous crime. It's nice to know my premonition was wrong."

"Perhaps you weren't wrong," John suggested. "Perhaps we just disturbed them and knowing we were on their trail prevented them from carrying out their purpose. We may only have delayed their unholy plan."

His companions were silent, considering this possibility and then Scarlet broke the silence. "I want to speak with this Edward Magnus," he growled. "It's time John and I had a chance to meet him."

"All right," Tuck nodded. The bad dreams had faded, his belly was full, and he was hopeful for the day to come. He smiled and led the way to the door, the others following behind him.

It was bitterly cold outside and the three wore their heavy winter cloaks which had the advantage of hiding John and Will's swords. It was not expressly forbidden to wear such weapons within the priory, indeed, the monks themselves carried knives, but it would not look good to have two burly strangers wandering around the grounds openly armed. There was no chance either man would leave their prized weapons in the guesthouse where they might be stolen, however, so they did their best to conceal them.

"Where should we start then?" Tuck asked cheerily, nodding a greeting to a pair of gloomy monks who were walking past on their way to turn the soil and add manure to the herb gardens in preparation for next spring's planting.

"Find the prior first?" John suggested. "Let him know exactly what we saw last night, without making any accusations. And then look for the cellarer and see if he can prove his whereabouts when the horses were taken?"

"Let's go then," Tuck smiled. "Maybe we can grab some cheese and even a bit of bacon on the way past the refectory too, eh?"

"Always hungry," Will laughed, ignoring sullen looks from another pair of monks who apparently did not share the positive feelings of the three friends.

Blaccalf's horses might not have been sacrificed, but the oppressive atmosphere still hung over Haltemprice like a heavy blanket.

Before they could take a step there was a rumble of hooves and a tired old horse rode in through the priory gates. The rider was young, dishevelled and wide-eyed and, from his ill-made clothing, Tuck took him for one of the local peasants.

"Help!" the youth cried out, doing his best to bring the horse to a halt although it was barely moving at a walk never mind a gallop. Sliding inelegantly to the ground, the rider cast about for someone to talk to and, quite to Tuck's amusement, ran to Will Scarlet.

"My lord," the young man begged, bowing his head and wringing his hands. "We need help. Something terrible's happened."

Will reached out and, with uncharacteristic gentleness, grasped the lad by the shoulders and looked at him reassuringly. "You're safe now," Scarlet told him in a firm voice. "Just slow down, and tell us what's wrong."

"You," Tuck called to one of the servants who was loitering nearby. "Fetch the prior, would you?"

The servant gave a curt nod, clearly irritated at missing out on the entertainment, but a look from Little John soon had him running for the main priory buildings.

"Our steading is a few miles to the west," the rider was saying to Will as Tuck turned his attention back to them. "Walkington, have you heard of it?"

"No," Scarlet replied. "We're not from around here. What brings you to the priory in this state, lad?"

"There's an old cemetery near our steading," the youth said. "It's full of Anglo-Saxon burials from hundreds of years ago. An ill-omened place. We locals avoid it as much as possible for the people buried there were said to be…" He trailed off, swallowing nervously and looking at Tuck as he murmured, "They were wicked folk. Unholy. Heathen!"

"How d'you know that?" John asked, not unkindly. "If they died hundreds of years ago."

"Everyone knows," the youngster replied, eyebrows raised as if he was astonished by the question. "It's just one of those things – legend passed down from generation to generation."

John pursed his lips but nodded, mollified. "Fair enough."

"What about the cemetery?" Will asked just as the glowering monk returned with the prior who recognised the young farmhand immediately and welcomed him with a worried frown, exhorting the lad to continue his tale.

"We passed the cemetery yesterday evening," the boy said. "It looked the same as normal. Grim and…" He trailed off, searching for the right word.

"Foreboding?" Tuck asked.

"Aye, that's it exactly, sir. Grim and foreboding. We hurried past it as fast as we could with the sheep. Even the dogs know not to stray too close to that place."

Tuck and John shared a look. If animals avoided a place it was a sure sign that something was wrong with it.

"Well, we come past there again this morning with the sheep, taking them to pasture, you know?" The boy met Will's gaze almost desperately, like a drowning man searching for some piece of flotsam to cling on to for dear life.

"I know," Scarlet agreed. "I'm a farmer myself nowadays."

"Well, the cemetery has been disturbed."

It took Tuck a moment to penetrate the lad's excited brogue but, when he did he felt a wave of revulsion wash over him. "Disturbed?" He demanded, outraged. Cemeteries were holy places!

"Aye, brother," the boy said, nodding furiously, eyes wide. "One of the old graves has been dug up. You can see the big pile of earth from the road."

Tuck made the sign of the cross and let out a long, fearful breath as the prior swore softly.

"As if this area wasn't cursed enough," Engayne muttered to himself. "This is all we need. Grave robbers."

"Why would anyone want to rob an ancient grave?" John wondered.

"Why would anyone want to sacrifice pigs on a hilltop?" Will Scarlet returned. "Who knows? Someone around here is up to no good though, that's obvious."

"Oh, Lord," Prior Engayne sighed, and Tuck noticed the man's wrinkled hands were shaking. "We must send word to the sheriff, and the bailiff, and put a stop to this blasphemy."

"Of course," Tuck agreed. "In the meantime, Father, I'll continue to look into these matters with John and Will, if you agree? Yes? Good. Then we'll accompany this lad back to his steading and take a look at the opened grave ourselves, eh, lads?"

John and Scarlet shared an apprehensive glance.

"I thought we were going to look for the—"

"Later, Will," Tuck broke in, cutting him off before he could mention the cellarer in front of Prior Engayne. "That can wait. Come on."

"Be careful," the prior warned as they bowed to him and moved off to collect their horses. "I fear whoever disturbed that grave and slaughtered the pigs is moon-touched, or simply evil. Who knows what else they're capable of?"

"Don't worry about us, Father," Little John replied grimly. "We're capable of plenty ourselves."

"Oh, I've no doubt of that," Engayne called after them as they approached the stables. "But I fear even you three have never faced anyone quite as dangerous as whoever's behind all this!"

TWELVE

The young farmhand knew the roads well and they made good time despite his old horse as they rode towards his steading. The air was crisp and cold and bit painfully at the exposed skin on the riders' hands and faces as they travelled.

"It's bloody freezing today," Will Scarlet grumbled as they rode. "Look," and he breathed out a cloud of steam.

"Well, it is almost Christmas," Tuck replied. "What d'you expect?"

"He's got a point though," John said, rummaging in his saddlebags before finally pulling out a pair of woollen mittens with a small cry of triumph. "It is much colder today. It's as if winter has suddenly arrived overnight."

"You got a spare pair of those mittens?" Scarlet asked hopefully. "I forgot to pack mine."

"So did I," John replied with a satisfied smile. "Amber packed these for me just as I was leaving."

"Clever woman, your wife," Tuck said, and he too was smiling for he'd also brought warm gloves along when he left Wakefield.

"We have spare mittens," the farmhand told Scarlet. "If you want to come to my steading first, rather than heading directly to the old cemetery."

Will thought about it for a moment but eventually shook his head. "Nah, I'd rather just get to the burial ground as soon as possible."

"You sure?" asked the farmhand just as flakes of snow began spiralling down from the overcast sky. "This looks like it might get heavy."

"No, it's fine," Scarlet told the youth whose name they'd discovered was Stephen. "If there's to be heavy snow we'd best get our business finished quickly and head back to the priory before the roads become impassable."

Such thoughts had not crossed any of their minds when they'd set out from Haltemprice but, looking up now, they saw the clouds were heavy and dark and the infernal wind had picked up yet again.

"Is it always like this here?" John asked, throwing up the hood of his cloak.

"The weather you mean?" asked the farmhand. "No, just the last few weeks it's turned strange. He looked around at the dreary landscape and shuddered.

"Interesting," the friar murmured, drawing his own cloak tighter around his neck and wishing he was indoors with a blazing fire and a warmed ale. "Are we nearly at the cemetery?"

"Aye, brother," Stephen nodded, patting his horse's neck as its hoof slipped momentarily on a damp, flat rock. "Just around the next bend and up a bit."

They travelled in silence as the temperature continued to drop and the road wound upwards, carrying them along a broader track which was clearly well used.

"Take care here," John said, eyeing the muddy ground anxiously. "There's churned hoofprints from horses, perhaps the ones that were stolen, as well as ruts from wagons. They've started to harden from the cold but could injure one of our horses' fetlocks, so let's move carefully."

"We're almost there," the farmhand told them. "We might be as well walking the horses from here anyway."

That seemed sensible and it was not long before they were at the wall which separated the ancient burial ground from the road. The horses were pegged firmly to the hardening ground but all four were skittish, as though they could sense something nearby that threatened them.

"Maybe one of us should stay here with the animals," Tuck suggested. "In case they decide to bolt. Those little pegs won't hold them for long."

"I'll wait," Stephen practically shouted. "I'd rather not go near those graves anyway. They're just there." He pointed and, sure enough, Tuck could make out a pile of earth marking the burial plot that had been dug open by the previous night's grave robbers.

"Saints preserve us," murmured the friar, blessing himself and following John and Will who had already scaled the wall and were making their way through the snow towards the grave.

"Wait." Scarlet grasped John's sleeve and pulled him to a halt, turning to wait for Tuck to catch up with them. "Maybe you should, you know, say a prayer or something. To protect us. This place has a bad feeling about it." His eyes roved about the ground warily, moving past the disturbed grave to take in the other burials, one or two of which were marked with lichened stone or rotting wooden crosses.

Friar Tuck strode up to them, grasping his pectoral cross in his left hand, quarterstaff in his right. "Good idea, Will," he said and carefully recited the Pater Noster. His friends murmured along with him and, although neither John nor Scarlet were deeply religious, they clearly took strength from the prayer. Indeed, it seemed to lift the oppressive atmosphere that hung so heavily across the burial ground and, when the three men moved on again they were filled with a rejuvenated sense of purpose.

"Come on, let's get this over with," said John, naturally assuming command since he was a bailiff, even if not of these particular lands.

They went to the pile of earth and stared down into the hole it had been dug from.

"There's nothing there," said Scarlet, leaning over to take a closer look.

John crouched beside him while Tuck recited another prayer, begging God to forgive them for further disturbing the final resting place of whoever had once been interred there.

"Not so much as a bone," John noted, even using his mittened hands to wipe away the thin layer of snow that had begun to form over the freshly dug earth.

"Whoever opened the grave took the skeleton that was here," Tuck said, voice shaking with barely controlled anger. "What blasphemy is this? To not only interfere with a burial site, but to remove the bones of the incumbent? This is sacrilegious beyond belief!"

"Or..." Scarlet said before trailing off and licking his lips nervously. "Perhaps whoever was buried here climbed out and just...walked away."

John and Tuck looked at one another at that, utterly aghast, before the huge bailiff snorted. "Don't be stupid, Will," he grated. "How could a dead man have dug himself out of his grave, leaving a neat pile of earth like that? He'd just have forced his way up and out, there'd be earth scattered in all directions."

"Exactly," Tuck said, relieved as he saw John's point. "Now, stop frightening yourself, Will. And us! Look," he nodded suddenly, eyes alighting on something stuck in the pile of excavated grave dirt. "What's that?"

John and Scarlet got to their feet and came to his side.

"Looks like a sword," Will said, forgetting his fear at the unexpected sight and reaching out to pull it from the earth. He shook it clean and rubbed it with his sleeve, revealing lettering engraved on the rusted old blade. "Can you read it, Tuck? I can't make it out."

Tuck squinted, rubbing with one of his mittens to clear even more of the earth away but the old weapon was in terrible condition, with the wooden handle completely gone and most of the blade broken off. "I think there was once a longer inscription on it," he said. "But now all I can make out is a name: Ecgbert. Presumably this was his sword, and his grave."

"Mother of God, this whole thing is really beginning to tear at my nerves," Scarlet growled as Tuck shoved the ancient blade back into the dirt.

"We should take a look at the rest of the burials," John said, stretching up and rolling his head from side to side to loosen tightened muscles. "See if they've been disturbed as well, or at least if we can find some clue to who's behind this vile desecration."

He and Scarlet hurried off to complete their search while Tuck squatted beside the empty grave. There was nothing to see there, but something else had caught his attention: a smell. He gingerly leaned down, putting his head into the six-foot deep hole while making sure he didn't slip and fall in. The scent was faint, whipped away in the fresh, icy air, but the friar immediately recognised it as the same one he'd smelled in Edward Magnus's underground lair.

As before, Tuck could not place the smell. It was unpleasant and aroused something deep within him although he knew not what. Was it part of the dreams he was enduring every night but could never fully remember upon waking? Or was he simply allowing his imagination to run away with itself? Hardly surprising given everything that had occurred since he'd first come to Haltemprice.

Whatever the odour came from, Tuck was absolutely certain it was connected in some way to the cellarer, Edward Magnus. The friar stood up, groaning slightly as his knees protested. "Find anything, boys?" he called as softly as possible while still being heard through the worsening snowfall.

"Nothing," John called, turning and striding back towards Tuck.

"Me neither," said Will, shaking his head in disappointment. "We've really got nothing at all to go on, have we? Anyone might have done this, although it seems obvious it was the men we saw last night. The poles on their backs weren't weapons – they were shovels."

"Indeed," said Tuck, leading the way back to the road. "And I noticed the same smell around the grave as I did in the undercroft where Edward Magnus works." The last word of his sentence was almost spat out in disgust.

"Then let's get back to the priory as soon as possible," John said, easily climbing over the wall and making for his horse which was pitifully happy to see him return.

"Good idea," Scarlet nodded as the gusting wind whipped down the hood of his cloak and he shouted a rather un-Christian oath at the sky.

Tuck said nothing as he joined them, pulling out the peg that tethered his palfrey to the frost- and snow-rimed ground. He dragged himself up into the saddle and turned to Stephen. "Lead the way, lad," he called.

"Right-o," the farmhand nodded, squinting into the snow as he nudged his horse ahead of them and started back westwards. "I'll leave you at the crossroads though, if that's all right, my lords? I'd dearly like to get home myself before the rising storm makes it impossible!"

THIRTEEN

"This is God punishing us all," Tuck cried, shouting to be heard over the storm that had grown in intensity since they'd left the young farmhand behind. "He's angry, and no wonder!"

Will Scarlet shouted something in return but his words were lost in the vicious, swirling wind. They could hardly see the length of themselves for the snow was now truly a blizzard and there was real fear amongst the men that they might not be able to find their way back to the priory. If they were caught out there in the open without anything to shelter beneath, or the ability to make a fire, well…Three pigs would not be the only bodies the residents of Haltemprice would have to deal with that month.

Tuck raised a hand to his brow, trying his best to keep the thick, white flakes from obscuring his vision. He was hoping to see a farmer's house, a barn, or even just a stand of trees to seek refuge beneath. A place where they could build a fire and stave off the onset of frostbite that threatened to maim, if not kill them all outright.

"This is not natural!" John roared, his great booming voice just barely carrying to Tuck who could only nod within his cloak in agreement.

The friar had travelled a great deal during his life, and not only in England. He had also spent many long months living outdoors in the forests of Nottingham and Yorkshire as an outlaw beside Will and John. Never before had he been caught in a storm such as this. It truly seemed as if something was trying to stop them from reaching safety.

A terrific gust buffeted the horses, sending them skittering to the side, whinnying in fear, and Tuck knew there was only one thing they could do to survive. "Our Father, which art in Heaven," he intoned, voice loud and strong. Despite the noise of the wind he realised his companions had heard him, for they joined in as he recited the rest of the prayer. When they finished there was no great miracle; the snow did not ease, the wind did not lessen, and no building to find solace in appeared before them. Tuck did feel his spirits rise though, and the cold did not seem to bother him quite so much.

He was suddenly reminded of Will's bare hands and moved his horse close to his friend's. "Here," he shouted, removing his own gloves and thrusting them at Scarlet. "You wear these for a time."

Will hesitated but Tuck could see the man's hands were already a fearful shade of blue.

"Take them!" the friar commanded. "Hurry up."

With a shout of thanks, Scarlet took the gloves. His hands were so numb that it took him a long moment of struggling to get them on but when he did he nodded at Tuck and they rode on in grim silence.

Little John led the way and the others followed. The bailiff knew northern England better than they did thanks to his occupation. He was not like most bailiffs – he did not oversee one particular village or town. Instead, the sheriff, Sir Henry de Faucumberg, employed John as more of a roving lawman, sending him from place to place hunting criminals or collecting fines from men who'd proved too troublesome or dangerous for the local bailiffs to deal with. He had passed through these lands before, and seemed to know where they should be going now.

"The priory is this way," John suddenly shouted and, because he was at the front the other two heard him. "I'm sure of it. Another mile and we'll be safe and warm!"

"Saints preserve us if you're wrong," Tuck murmured as another terrific blast of wind almost knocked his palfrey off its hooves.

They plodded slowly onwards, the horses struggling to walk through the deepening white carpet that looked so pretty but would kill them all before long if they could not escape its icy grip.

What on Earth is going on here in Haltemprice? Tuck wondered, staring at the snow so hard that he felt blinded by it. Nothing else could be seen but those insidious falling flakes and the friar did his best to keep his mind working by going over the events of the past few days.

Edward Magnus was surely the key. He was the one studying dark magics. The one man who seemed to be truly enjoying the bleak atmosphere that lay across the priory. The one man who had threatened Tuck.

"Wake up!"

Will Scarlet's voice roused the friar from the stupor he'd fallen into and Tuck almost lashed out at his friend. He'd been so warm and comfortable, drifting away into a much-needed sleep until Will brought him rudely back to wakefulness and this world of endless, freezing white.

"You can't go to sleep, Tuck," Scarlet was shouting at him. "You'll die! Here!" The gloves were removed and now Will guided his horse close and forced the frost-covered items onto the friar's hands. "Are we nearly there yet, John? We can't go on like this for much longer."

John glanced back over his shoulder. He may not have heard Will's question but he guessed what it was from the state of Tuck. "I don't know," he roared over another howling gust. "I pray so."

Tuck almost laughed at his giant friend's face. It bore an expression of hopelessness, but what seemed so amusing to the friar was the white coat that had covered John's grizzled beard, making him look about fifty years older than his thirty-seven winters.

"Tuck won't make it much farther," Scarlet shouted. "We must find shelter, John. Now!"

"Where?" John demanded, casting an arm about at the blizzard. "I can barely see my own hand in front of me! Nottingham Castle could be right beside us and we wouldn't know."

We're going to die here, Tuck thought to himself and, strangely, he felt no fear, only a sense of calm. It would be good to slide down from his palfrey and fall asleep in the inviting white blanket beneath.

But then he thought of Edward Magnus and anger boiled up within the friar. No, he did not want to rest – he wanted to discover what the cellarer was doing! He wanted to know why the pigs had been sacrificed, and why the ancient sorcerer Ecgbert's bones had been stolen.

Please, God, guide us back to the priory, he prayed. *Please, let us discover what the cellarer is doing, and put a stop to it!*

There was another great blast of wind, even stronger than any that had come before, and Tuck realised he was lying in the snow, staring up at the endless falling flakes. There was no pain, no shock, only the barest hint of surprise and then, mercifully, he drifted away and felt nothing more.

FOURTEEN

"Move back please, my lord!" The infirmarian was small and wizened, but he seemed to have great strength in his slim frame as he herded Little John back from the bed that Friar Tuck was lying upon. "Let me do my work, please."

The bailiff towered over the monk, but he bowed his head and lifted his hands in apology as he stepped away from the bed and headed for the door where Will Scarlet was already standing.

"I'll send word for you when I have news," the infirmarian promised. "Now, out, and shut the door behind you."

With a last, sorrowful glance at Tuck, John went into the corridor and stood with his back against the wall, gazing up at the ceiling. The intricate carvings overhead were lost on the bailiff who could only focus on the terrible mental image of his old friend, blue-lipped, deathly pale, and cold to the touch.

"Do you think he'll be all right?" Scarlet asked in an uncharacteristically subdued tone. "Will that skinny monk be able to help him?"

John let out a long sigh and glanced down at Will. "I don't know," he said. "But there's nothing we can do here and, I don't know about you, but I'm bloody freezing myself. Let's find a fire if we can in this place, and some food."

When Tuck fell off his horse neither John nor Will Scarlet had noticed for quite some time. Miraculously, however, they had come upon

Haltemprice Priory's gatehouse soon after and, after celebrating their delivery from certain death, only then had they realised Tuck was not with them, just his palfrey.

Despite being practically frozen to the bone the two friends had immediately trudged back out into the howling storm to search for the missing friar. For what seemed like hours they wandered, calling out as despair grew within them. And then, miraculously, a little red-breasted robin had landed in front of them and, recognising it as a sign, they had followed the bird that did not seem to be bothered by the gusting wind or blinding snow.

They'd soon found Tuck, and John had thrown him over his shoulder and carried him into the priory with a prayer of thanks to God and the robin on his cracked lips.

The door to the building had been locked when they reached it, and after much hammering by Scarlet it was opened by Prior Engayne himself. He had immediately ordered stablehands to take care of the three exhausted horses standing inside the gates, and then led John and Will to the infirmary where elderly and sickly monks were taken care of. Engayne had disappeared while they were speaking with the infirmarian, but he returned now.

"You two," he barked, his natural leadership coming to the fore. "Follow me, I have food and ale ready for you."

"Forgive me, Father," said John, whose teeth were chattering almost uncontrollably by now. "I think we'd prefer a blazing fire first, if that'd be possible."

The prior halted and looked up at the bailiff, then at Will. "Of course," he agreed. "The calefactory is just along here."

"Calefactory?" John asked, confused.

"Warming house," Scarlet told him, furiously rubbing his arms in an attempt to heat up. "But, Father, that will be full of monks during this storm, won't it? It might be better if we warmed ourselves somewhere a bit more private, so we can let you know what we found at the old cemetery without anyone overhearing us."

The prior frowned and eyed him almost suspiciously for a time as though he wondered why their tidings should be kept secret. Soon enough though, he nodded and changed direction. "All right, this way then. I'll take you to my own quarters. I have a fire there, and I can have a servant bring you refreshments. No one will overhear what you have to tell me in my own rooms."

Prior Engayne's personal rooms were not as lavish as some. Will had told John that the heads of some religious orders lived in large, expensively decorated houses within the grounds of their abbeys or monasteries. The rooms that the prior ushered Will and John into were comfortable and quite large, but not ostentatious and, like much of the building, construction had not yet been fully completed. Most importantly though, there was a fire burning in the hearth and a servant added a log to it before hurrying out to fetch food and drink for the men.

"This weather is just vile," the prior said, standing and looking out of the window at the snow. As if in reply, the wind battered the glass and Engayne shrank back, turning to chuckle self-consciously at his visitors. "Never seen anything like it, I must say."

He sat down and the men waited, John and Will shaking the snow off their cloaks before warming themselves gratefully by the fire until the servant returned with three cups of ale and a trencher of cheese, bread, and sausage.

"Please, fill your bellies," the prior said, smiling and tilting his head gracefully as he gestured towards the food. "We're lucky you two did not succumb to the weather like Brother Tuck."

The two guests did not need a second invitation for they were absolutely famished. The journey through the snow had utterly drained them, and the generous repast went some way to restoring them to full health, in body, if not quite in mind.

The servant was dismissed once the meal was over and he left the chamber with the empty trencher, latching the door behind him.

"Now, gentlemen," said Engayne, lifting the poker from beside the hearth and placing it into the flames. "If you're up to it, perhaps you would tell me what happened this morning when you rode out from the priory?"

John looked at Will who nodded and held out his palm, prompting the bailiff to take the lead. Scarlet might have once been a monk for a short time, but John was a representative of the sheriff, even if he was visiting Haltemprice in an unofficial capacity.

"Well, there's not much to tell regarding the old cemetery," the lawman stated, nodding thankfully as the prior took the poker from the fire and gestured towards John's cup of ale.

The liquid steamed when the red-hot iron was plunged in and the bailiff took a sip, a low groan of pleasure escaping his lips before he continued his account of the morning's events.

"As the young farmhand said, one of the graves had been disturbed."

"Emptied," Will Scarlet put in.

"Emptied?" the prior asked, brow furrowed in shock.

"Well, we assume so," John confirmed. "The grave had been dug out but there were no bones, no grave goods, nothing at all other than an old broken sword. If someone was buried there, their remains have been removed."

"But why?" Prior Engayne asked, shaking his head and placing the poker back into the fire to heat again. "What kind of a monster steals the bones of the dead? And for what purpose?"

Neither John nor Will wanted to speculate, although both men had their own ideas of what the grave robbers might want with the ancient skeleton, and Tuck had alluded to even darker reasons driving the thieves without going into detail.

"Who knows?" said John with an expansive shrug. "It's all very sinister."

"Sinister indeed!" Engayne cringed as yet another gust rattled the window frames. "Do you have any idea who might be behind it all?"

Again, the visitors shared a look, unwilling to accuse Edward Magnus of such heinous crimes. Sacrificing pigs to the devil and violating graves was enough for a man to be excommunicated, if not hanged. Without proof, no action could be taken against the cellarer though.

"We're not really sure," John hedged.

"Although," Will added as the prior heated his ale with the poker, "Tuck had wanted to speak with your cellarer before we went off to visit the old cemetery."

"Brother Magnus?" the prior asked and his expression was blank, his tone unreadable.

"Aye, Father," Will said, his voice equally level. "Tuck said the cellarer has a great collection of interesting books. Maybe he thought they'd be of use in the investigation."

The prior looked from one to the other and, although he did his best not to betray his thoughts, the very fact that he was masking his emotions told its own story.

"Very well," Engayne said, clasping his hands and standing up. "Have you met Brother Magnus yet?"

"No," John replied with a slight shake of the head.

"Then I shall take you to him if you're quite rested? Good, follow me." He led the way out into the corridor which felt cold and draughty after the cosiness of his personal quarters. All three men pulled their cloaks up and hurried towards their destination. The cloister, when they reached it, was also bitterly cold and not a single monk was there.

"Father?" A voice called out from the opposite end of the walkway. "Father, may I have a word with you?"

"What is it?" the prior retorted a little irritably. "Trouble in the kitchen again, no doubt," he murmured to John and Will from the side of his mouth. "It's so hard to find good staff these days."

"We seem to be short of some things," the servant called back apologetically. "I think the last delivery must have been light."

"God's body," Engayne hissed, glaring at the man but speaking again to John and Will Scarlet. "I'll wager someone signed for that delivery without checking it properly. Damn it, I had better go and see to this." He pointed towards a door. "That leads to the undercroft. There is a very good chance you'll find the cellarer down there. It should not be locked. Will you be all right to go down yourselves? You can borrow a lantern, or a candle from the library there."

John nodded as Engayne pointed at a second door. "We'll find our way, Father, thank you."

"It'll be absolutely freezing; you might want to get another cloak." The prior gave a little chuckle as he headed off towards the kitchen, calling over his shoulder, "Or perhaps a blanket!"

"I'm sure we'll manage," Scarlet muttered as the pair went to the library. He opened the door and immediately apologised for two monks were wrapped in layers of heavy blankets, hard at work copying out books. They glared at him as he came into the room.

"There," John whispered to him in a comically loud voice. "The candle, you idiot. Grab it!"

Will did so and then bowed his head at the irritated scribes, backing out the door, candle gripped in his hand like a sword.

"How the hell can they write in this cold?" John demanded, muffling laughter as they headed towards the entrance to the undercroft.

"They're used to it I expect," Will replied, grinning. "I don't envy them."

The undercroft was, as Prior Engayne suggested, unlocked, and they went inside, closing the door behind them to keep the worst of the wind out. They had planned on using flint and steel to light the borrowed candle but, as they stood on the top step, eyes adjusting to the gloom, they realised that it was not entirely dark in the undercroft.

John placed a hand on his lips and nodded downwards. "Someone's there," he said. "Best move quietly or we'll upset them like we did those two in the library."

Will nodded assent and the pair went down the stairs side by side, feeling the temperature drop even further as they went.

As they reached the bottom they began walking straight ahead, towards the room where Tuck had told them Edward Magnus liked to work. Before they'd taken half a dozen steps, however, three men appeared from one of the side rooms and blocked their way.

John opened his mouth to greet them, and then he realised these were not simple monks. Their hair had not been shaved into tonsures, they did not wear black robes, and they did not look like the type to spend their days in prayer and contemplation.

To make matters worse, all three of the men were tall, well-built, and held long-bladed knives in their hands.

FIFTEEN

"Who the hell are you?" The nearest of the three men demanded. He had protruding eyes and a marked underbite which combined to give him a sinister appearance, as if the blade in his grubby fist didn't already do that.

"Visitors to the priory," John replied levelly. He did not particularly like the idea of fighting these three, especially in the cramped confines of the dimly-lit corridor. "I'm a bailiff," he added.

"I don't give a shit if you're the Sheriff of Nottingham himself," the man with the underbite growled. "You're not allowed down here."

"The prior himself told us to come down here to see the cellarer," Will Scarlet said in a voice as cold as the frost outside. "So get out of the way before we take those knives and shove them right up your arses."

Used to dealing with monks, the other two men were clearly surprised to be challenged like this, expecting the newcomers to turn tail and flee. The fact that Will and John were confidently standing up to them, and looked as immovable as the flaring stone columns that supported the ceiling, had visibly rattled them. Their leader, the one with the protruding lower jaw, was not about to stand aside, however.

"We don't answer to the prior," he said. "The cellarer employs us himself, and he doesn't like people down here. There's a lot of valuable stuff in this undercroft."

"Aye, food and wine and things like that," one of his companions put in, his voice nowhere near as composed as the leader's. John marked that one as a weak link – if it came to a fight he would deal with the other two first.

"What d'you mean the cellarer 'employs' you?" Scarlet demanded, visibly outraged. "Monks aren't supposed to have any personal wealth."

"Maybe so," the leader chuckled. "But I'm not working for him for free."

"Well, I don't care who you answer to," Scarlet returned. "The prior is in charge of Haltemprice, not the cellarer, and not you three ugly bastards! Now get out of the way."

"He's right," John nodded, smiling a little to try and offset his friend's hard words. "You wouldn't want to prevent an officer of the law from going about his business, would you? The cellarer can't be paying you enough to make it worth your trouble."

The man with the underbite curled his lip and spat on the floor between them. "I might have let you past, but your friend there is a cheeky twat. I don't feel like doing anything he says, so…" He trailed off and lifted his knife higher. "Get back up those stairs unless you want this in your guts, lawman."

"You two in on this as well?" John demanded, suddenly straightening up to his full height, his demeanour changing in an instant from calm and reasonable to terrifying. He glared at the men standing just behind the one with the underbite. They were both taller than their leader, but younger, less grizzled, and far less confident. Still, they did not lower their weapons or back away, and John let out a low growl as he said to Will, "You ready, Scarlet? I think we're going to have to go through these fools."

"Get them!" the enemy leader roared, lunging forward with his blade.

John had not yet drawn either his own sword or knife but he side-stepped the wild thrust and brutally slammed his opponent's head into the wall. "You little bastard," he roared, great voice echoing along the narrow corridor as he looked down at his torn cloak. "You cut me!"

Will was not idle either – as the enemy leader crashed into the wall Scarlet punched him full in the face, so hard that it might well have righted his underbite. It was a vicious blow, throwing the man backwards onto the ground, the back of his skull making a horrible cracking sound that let everyone know his part in the fight was over.

John was not in the mood to try and negotiate any further with the other two who still barred their way. He stepped forward, Will at his side, and both drew their swords. The remaining foes, terrified by what had happened to their leader, dropped their knives, the blades clattering loudly on the hard floor.

"Not so hard now, are you?" Will Scarlet demanded, and it looked like he might actually attack the unarmed men but John reached out and grasped his arm.

"They're no threat," the bailiff said soothingly, waiting until Scarlet's temper was under control again before releasing his volatile friend's sleeve and addressing the frightened men. "Are you?"

The two lay servants – for John recognised them now as men he'd seen working in the herb garden and unloading a wagon of produce the day before – shook their heads and backed into the room they'd appeared from.

"Good. Drop those knives and kick them over to me. Now!"

The servants did as they were told, jumping at John's great bellow and skittering further back into the room which was lit by a number of candles.

"Sit down," John commanded as Will followed him inside. It was a medium-sized room, with just a couple of wooden boxes and barrels which John did not bother to examine, assuming they contained merely food and drink. There were stools which the captives sat down on, eyeing the open doorway warily, perhaps thinking of making a run for it. Handily, there were two long lengths of rope lying beside the boxes and John used his sword to slice it into sections which he dropped on the ground. "Here, Scarlet. Bind them."

Will sheathed his own sword and lifted a piece of the rope. "Arms behind your back," he ordered the first servant who hesitated only until Scarlet grabbed him by the throat and squeezed, commanding him once again to do as he was told.

It was not long before both the servants were securely bound hand and foot, and then John dragged the third, unconscious man into the room and Will tied him up too.

"We should take these candles," Scarlet suggested. "Clearly, the cellarer isn't in here, so we'll need light to go looking for him."

"You won't find him," one of the servants said, a note of triumph on his face. Even a small victory was something, it seemed.

"Where is he?" John asked, standing threateningly over the bound men. "We're in no mood for games. Our friend is close to death in the infirmary, and I'll put you in the same place if you don't tell us where Brother Magnus is!"

"We don't know," one of them said. He was a stocky man, balding, with long grey hair that hung about his shoulders. "He comes and goes where he will. Sometimes he's busy down here, other times he's about his business as the cellarer."

"And what are you three arseholes doing down here?" Scarlet demanded and, although his sword was back in its scabbard, his demeanour was as menacing as ever.

"Guarding his things."

"What things?" John asked.

"Just the things he has down here," the balding man replied evasively.

"Bones?" hissed Scarlet. "From an ancient grave that you lot violated last night, after riding there on stolen horses? Or maybe parts of the pigs you stole from the farm and sacrificed to the devil?"

John watched the faces of the two prisoners as Will spoke and noted the fear that bloomed as soon as the blasphemous crimes were mentioned. These men knew exactly what Will was talking about, and their fear quickly turned to panic which they did their best to mask.

"Where is Magnus?" Little John growled, leaning down on his haunches and touching the point of his sword to the balding man's throat. "You know who we are, don't you?"

The servant swallowed, wincing as his Adam's apple was pricked by the sharpened steel.

"I'm John Little, and he's Will Scarlet. I'm sure you've heard what we do to people who get on the wrong side of us."

One of the bound men was so frightened that a dark stain blossomed on his breeches. John turned his attention to him, standing over him like an executioner. This servant was lean and bore a long scar from his temple to his jaw, but he did not look so much like a soldier now as he cowered down on the stool.

"Tell us where the cellarer is, and what you've all been up to, and I'll make sure the sheriff is lenient with you."

"I don't know," the frightened servant gasped, staring up pleadingly at the bailiff. "He locks himself in the room at the end of the corridor and works alone while we stay out here making sure no one disturbs him."

"You were with him when the swine were sacrificed?" Scarlet asked. "And when the grave was robbed last night?"

The scarred man glanced at his balding companion before both looked at the floor and hung their heads in silence.

"It's not important just now," John said to Will. "We should arrest Brother Magnus. These three can confess once we have the cellarer safely in custody."

Scarlet set about tying more lengths of rope around the mouths of the prisoners so they couldn't call for help. If some monk stumbled upon them he might untie them and they could make their escape so, a short time later all three were bound and gagged, and the unconscious servant was slowly coming to.

"Come on," John said to Will. "Let's grab those candles and get this over with."

"Wait!" Although the servant with the scarred face had a length of rope tied around his head and his words were muffled John could just make them out. "Don't leave us alone in here in the dark. Please!"

"God's bollocks," Scarlet muttered, shaking his head at the terror-stricken man. "Afraid of the dark now too?"

They went out of the room and headed for the chamber at the end of the corridor, the candles they'd taken with them casting malevolent shadows on the walls and ceiling columns as they walked in silence. In the pitch-black room behind them the captives moaned and howled fearfully, setting John's frayed nerves even more on edge than they already were.

"This whole priory is…" Scarlet trailed off, looking nervously behind him as they neared the cellarer's chamber.

"I know," John replied in a hushed tone. "It seems cursed."

"Aye," Scarlet agreed, chewing his lip as they halted at the closed door and looked at one another, swords in hand. "And this room is at the centre of it all."

John's hand came up and he lifted the latch to Brother Magnus's work room. Throwing any caution to the wind – they'd come to find a bookish monk after all, not a warrior – Will Scarlet slammed his shoulder against the door and charged into the room with Little John close behind him.

A gust of icy air whistled into the chamber ahead of them, blowing a small pile of dust or salt off a desk.

"By Christ, it's absolutely freezing down here," Scarlet shivered, eyes casting about for some sign of the cellarer.

"It is," John agreed. "As if the walls don't keep out the wind properly or something."

"Where is the bastard? Don't tell me he's not even in here after all that trouble in the corridor."

They searched the room, breath steaming in the candlelight, but it was clear Brother Magnus was not there. The place was too small to hide in and the furniture – desk, bookcase, a couple of chairs, and even the metallic apparatus that baffled them as much as it had Tuck – could not be used to conceal something as big as a man.

The muffled sound of monks singing overhead filtered through the ceiling then, while in the room they'd just left the captives renewed their frightened moaning, making John and Will glance at one another uncomfortably. Why were three grown men so scared of the dark? They should be more afraid of the King's justice! And yet, John understood the terrified grunts carrying to them from the darkness behind. The thought of being bound hand and foot and left alone down here without a light…The bailiff shuddered and gripped the hilt of his sword tighter as they continued to search the cellarer's chamber for a clue that might point to his complicity in the recent nefarious events.

"What's that smell?" John asked as he lifted books and ink and other things from the table, hoping to see something incriminating. "You smell that?"

Scarlet turned away from the book case and sniffed the air noisily before screwing up his face. "I don't know what that is. It smells...old. Fusty and old."

"I think it's this stuff." John dropped to one knee and ran the tip of a finger through the dust that had been swept off the desk when the wind blew in. He raised it to his nose and breathed in, nodding sourly as he did so. "It is, but I've no idea what it might be."

"Better not touch it too much," Will advised, looking anxiously about the room as the muffled singing from the church above grew louder. "God himself only knows what the cellarer gets up to in here. I wouldn't be surprised if that dust used to be one of the bones in the grave that was robbed! Maybe that's what he uses those copper tubes and stuff for."

It was supposed to be a light-hearted comment, not serious, but as Scarlet said it John felt a shiver run through him and he hastily wiped the dust off his finger and rose back to his feet.

"This place is hellish," the bailiff said in a low voice. "There's nothing for us to find here, and the cellarer is away so we might as well return to the prior; let him know we've taken those servants into custody and to send a messenger telling the local bailiff to hurry up and get here."

"At least those three have given up their moaning," Scarlet said, heading for the passageway but continually looking over his shoulder as he went, as though he half expected someone, or something, to attack him even though they knew the chamber was empty. He allowed John to lead, and closed the door firmly behind them as they made their way back towards the steps that would carry them up to fresh, clean air once more.

The Gregorian chant had finished overhead and, as they passed the room with the captives in it, John stuck his head inside, holding up the candle and peering at the bound men. They stared back at him, silent now, as though they'd accepted their fate.

"Good," the bailiff said. "You can stay here for a while until we find the cellarer, and Prior Engayne brings the law."

They eyed him sullenly but made no sound, not pleading for mercy or release, or hurling muffled insults at their captors. That was perhaps even more disconcerting than the earlier mumbling and groaning and John backed out of the room, sudden realisation striking him as he noticed blood pooling on the undercroft floor around the three servants.

"What's wrong?" Will asked, immediately noting John's shock as he came back into the passageway. "Are they all right?"

"No," the bailiff replied, stunned. "They're all dead!"

SIXTEEN

A novice was passing as John and Will climbed the stairs from the undercroft and emerged into the daylight. They could see the sky, heavy, grey, and menacing, but the snow had stopped for a time at least and it was a relief to breathe fresh, clean air again.

Shocked, they'd confirmed the servants were all dead, suffering stab wounds to the front and back from an unknown assailant while they lay, bound, gagged, and utterly defenceless. No wonder they'd been moaning so desperately.

"Boy, does this door lock?" Will Scarlet called hoarsely to the novice who gaped at them as if he'd never seen their like before.

Which might be true, John supposed – there weren't many people as tall as him after all. Or as angry as Scarlet, whose infamous temper seemed to have escalated even higher than normal as a result of the sinister atmosphere and the sense of lurking fear that encompassed the priory's environs. Finding dead bodies hadn't done much for his disposition either.

"I think so," the boy replied uncertainly, clearly unsure how to address this pair of dangerous-looking warriors who might have just stumbled into the cloister after a tavern brawl. "But, if it does, the cellarer will have the key."

"Damn that cellarer," Scarlet grumbled then, louder, "where is he? Have you seen him?"

The novice shook his tonsured head.

"What about the prior? You seen him?"

Again, the novice shook his head, and John got the impression they could have spent all day asking the youth questions and receiving only a shake of the head in reply, no matter what they asked.

"For God's sake," Scarlet said, throwing his hands in the air as he turned a despairing eye on his huge friend. "Now what?"

"You," John said, jerking his chin towards the novice and using his most commanding tone. "Stand guard here at this door. No one is to go in or out, do you understand?" He did not openly threaten the lad, but his bleak gaze made it quite clear there would be trouble if his orders were not followed to the letter. "If the prior comes by, tell him we're looking for him."

The boy gaped at them but his previous, dull expression had transformed. Excitement! This was something different to the usual routine of the priory, and the novice was fully invested. He nodded vigorously. "I'll make sure no one goes into the cellar, sir," he vowed grimly, hand falling to the knife at his waist. "Or comes out."

John nodded approvingly. "Good man," he said, his words having the desired effect as the novice's shoulders squared and he practically saluted the huge bailiff.

Will led as the two companions moved around the cloister and through the inner passageways towards the infirmary. They were not challenged for this section of the priory seemed to be deserted, the majority of the monks seeking shelter and warmth in the few parts of the complex that had fires burning.

The infirmary itself was unlocked and the pair went in, steeling themselves for the worst. It had been preternaturally cold that morning when they'd become lost in the storm – had Tuck's fall into the snow been too much for his body to take? He was not elderly yet, but he had faced many physical tribulations over the years, being beaten, stabbed, and even shot with a crossbow bolt by Sir Guy of Gisbourne. Certainly, Tuck's life had not been one of peace, solitude and quiet contemplation, and both John and Will Scarlet feared this latest adventure would prove fatal for their old friend.

The infirmarian saw them coming through the door and hurried over, rubbing his hands to try and force some warmth into them. There was a fire in the large chamber but with the high ceilings and constant draughts coming through gaps in the window frames it was not quite cosy.

"How's our friend?" Will asked, worry making his words clipped and harsh in the peace of the infirmary.

The wizened little surgeon looked at them for a breathless moment and then he blessed them with a beatific smile. "The friar is absolutely fine," he said. "In fact, we gave him some warm broth and he's now up and about, as bright as a new penny."

Both John and Will grinned at the news and, when Tuck himself appeared from behind a column they all shared a rough embrace as the infirmarian looked on in surprise. Such hard men as these did not often show their emotions so openly, but John did not care what anyone thought. Their time as outlaws, living a hair's breadth from death every single day, had made the three friends fully appreciate each day alive on God's green earth.

Even if it was mostly white at the moment, the bailiff thought ruefully, looking out through one of the windows and seeing that the snow was falling once more.

"Did you find who we were looking for?" Tuck asked.

"No," Will replied in disgust. "But we were attacked by three of his servants."

"More fool them," Tuck noted drily. He was pale and his face was drawn but apart from that he appeared unharmed by the morning's ordeal.

"They're all dead," John told him.

"What?" Tuck fought to keep his voice low but he was plainly furious.

"It wasn't us," Will hissed. "We tied them up – alive – and left them in one of the undercroft rooms. When we came back a short time later they'd been stabbed to death."

"Oh, Holy Father," Tuck groaned, dipping his head and clasping his hands as he prayed for the souls of the departed, and for his friends who would surely be blamed for the murders.

"They were in on it," John said. "That's why Magnus has had them silenced. We need to find that bastard, and force him to tell us what he knows."

"Then what are we waiting for?" Tuck asked, although without his usual effusiveness. "Let's clear your names, and put an end to all this for good."

SEVENTEEN

Tuck, John, and Will hurried back to the cloister where they found the novice still on guard, a fierce scowl on his face. He was shivering, however, making him look rather less frightening than he probably hoped.

"Anyone bother you?" John asked, the hint of a smile touching his lips.

"No, lord," the boy replied through chattering teeth. "Not a soul passed."

"Good lad," the bailiff said. "Go and find a fire and some warmed ale. Thank you for your help."

"And if you see the prior, tell him we need to talk with him," Will added as the boy hurried off, clasping his blue hands and blowing into them, cold but clearly satisfied with a job well done.

"Merciful Christ," John said as the boy disappeared through one of the doors that led off from the cloisters. "I know the windows are glazed, or have at least been shuttered, but it's absolutely bitter. How do the monks work in here every day in the winter?"

Tuck shrugged. "It's not always snowing and blowing a gale. Besides, this is the life the brothers choose. They forgo luxury, and live in poverty without the comforts the likes of you two enjoy."

"Ha!" Will gave a sarcastic bark of laughter, although whether it was a comment on Tuck's lifestyle, which was very much like those of his two friends, or on that of the monks in the priory who lived a life of ease compared to most people in England, John was not sure.

"Ah, there you are! And Brother Tuck back on his feet, God be praised."

The three men turned to see the prior coming towards them.

"Good timing," said Tuck with a shallow bow of his head. "Come with us, please, Father. We have something to show you, and much to tell."

Prior Engayne looked terribly harassed and it was plainly obvious that matters were taking a toll on him. He eyed the three friends in turn, drew in a deep breath, and nodded stoically. "Lead on then," he said. "At least we'll get away from that damnable wind for a time in the undercroft."

"I wouldn't be so sure about that," John told him as they went down to the cellar, retrieving the candles they'd left on the stairs and waiting a moment for Will to get them lit with his flint and steel. "There was a terrible draught when we were down here before."

"A draught?" the prior asked, a quizzical frown on his face. "But there are no windows down here. We're underground."

John shrugged. "I was surprised myself, but it was quite a strong draught. Maybe it comes through the door from the cloisters."

"Maybe," Prior Engayne conceded. "But I've never noticed it before when I've been down here. Strange. Much like many of the things that have been happening here since we moved in!"

John grunted. Strange was an understatement, and things were about to get even stranger for the prior.

They reached the room with the prisoners inside and John entered first, candle held aloft.

"What the..." Prior Engayne peered around Tuck's portly figure and pressed a hand to his mouth, eyes bulging. "Is that some of our servants? Are they...?"

"Aye," Scarlet ground out in a voice as deep and dark as the undercroft itself. "They're all dead, but it wasn't us!"

Prior Engayne was visibly shocked and Tuck supported him until he regained his equilibrium. The four of them stood for a long, breathless moment, staring at the dead men, and then the prior looked up at Little John and, to the bailiff's amazement, drew out a knife.

EIGHTEEN

"It's all right, Father!" Friar Tuck grabbed hold of the prior and quickly, expertly disarmed him. "You're safe with us."

"Safe?" Prior Engayne demanded, rubbing his wrist where Tuck had twisted it. "Safe?" he cried again. "Your friends have murdered three of my servants!"

"Of course they haven't," Tuck replied in a level but hard voice. "Think, Father. John Little is a bailiff. I am a friar. Will Scaflock…" He trailed off, knowing all too well the old tales that circulated about Scarlet's brutality, many of them genuine. "Well," Tuck finished a little lamely, "you can trust us."

"Thanks, Tuck," Will snorted and bent to examine the wounds on the dead men. "You smell that?"

John nodded, kneeling beside him. "That same stench we noticed at the old graveyard."

"That smell is always here," Prior Engayne said, slowly recovering from his momentary fright. "It seems to accompany Brother Magnus wherever he goes – something to do with his studies, I believe."

"What the hell is it?" Scarlet asked, wafting a hand in front of his face and edging towards the door as though he wanted to get far away from the noisome chamber.

"I know not," the prior admitted softly. "It may be from a grey powder, or dust, that I've noticed he carries with him at times."

"We saw that too," John broke in, pointing down the corridor towards the cellarer's work room. "In there."

"Exactly," Engayne nodded. His demeanour was stiff, as if he was still not entirely convinced that he wasn't in danger himself. He shook his head, casting another shuddering glance at the three corpses that stared back from terrible, glassy eyes.

A sudden realisation struck John then, lost until now in the excitement.

"These three could have told us what Edward Magnus was up to down here," he said. "They were all in on it – the pig sacrifices, the grave robbing – they told us as much. Without them though, we have no case against him."

"True," Will growled. "And that, at least, points us in the direction of the killer. Only Magnus had a motive to murder these idiots."

"But why would he?" Tuck asked, confused. "How would he know you'd arrested them and held them here, unless he was down here too, and heard you talking with them?"

The men stood for a silent moment in the oppressive undercroft, minds racing, trying to understand what on God's Earth was happening in Haltemprice Priory.

"This is insane," Will muttered. "This whole bloody place is insane. No offence, Father."

"None taken," Prior Engayne replied dourly. "It's hard to disagree with you!"

"Come on," said Tuck, handing the prior his knife back with an apologetic smile. "Let's get out of here before we all go mad."

"First, let's check the work room at the end of the passage," John said, the methodical lawman in him coming to the fore again. "Just in case the cellarer is hiding in there."

Drawing his sword once more, Will led the way and Tuck hung back with the prior as they made entry into Edward Magnus's chamber, but it was as empty as it had been before.

"Damn it," Will grumbled. "I was hoping he'd be here and we could see an end to this for good."

"No such luck," said John. "But wait." He licked a finger and held it up. "You feel that? There's the draught again." He looked at the prior who nodded, nonplussed.

"You're right, bailiff," he admitted. "But where is it coming from?"

For a time they moved about the chamber trying to work out where the wind was blowing through from but, in the end, they were forced to give up. The draught seemed to be coming from more than one direction and, with no windows or doors other than the one they'd just come through, the mystery remained unsolved.

* * *

"I don't understand why you believe Brother Magnus is involved in all this."

Prior Engayne had taken the three visitors back to his own chambers where they could talk in private with the fire to warm them and some strong wine to fortify their spirits. The day had been a shocking one, even for the former outlaws who were more used to sudden or even violent deaths than the monks. "What possible reason could you have to accuse him so?"

John and Will looked at Tuck for, in truth, they were not sure how to answer the prior – they had still never even met the cellarer, yet they were somehow as convinced of the man's guilt as the friar.

"His servants threatened me when I was in the undercroft," Tuck said.

"That reflects badly on them," the prior noted. "Not Brother Magnus."

"There's also the smell," Tuck went on. "I noticed it on the hill where the pigs were sacrificed, again in the undercroft where Magnus works, and yet again in the defiled grave. You said yourself that the smell seems to emanate from Brother Magnus, or at least from something he works with."

The prior took that in and then shook his head, lips pursed as he stared at Tuck. "A smell. That's not enough to convict a man of these heinous crimes."

"The three men in the undercroft as good as confessed to us that they were involved with Magnus," John pointed out.

"'As good as confessed'?" Prior Engayne returned with a short laugh of disbelief. "Come now, John. You're a bailiff. You know that it takes rather more evidence than that to prove someone's guilt. Besides, those servants cannot testify against Brother Magnus now, can they?"

"Conveniently enough for the cellarer," Will noted.

"Indeed," the prior agreed. "But it leaves us with nothing. You must find out more before the law will move against Brother Magnus." He shook his head, a mixture of emotions crossing his face like the storm clouds that were scudding across the sky outside. "I understand Edward likes to delve into strange books, and knows some things that would make any normal man shudder, but would he go so far as to murder three men? And what about this damnable weather and feeling of unease that hangs over the whole priory? Is that his fault too?"

"You know the murdered servants were being paid by Brother Magnus?"

The prior's face darkened at that. "With what? The monks have no personal wealth or possessions, or at least they're not supposed to. Even the books in Magnus's library belong to the priory, officially."

"He must be getting money from somewhere," Will said. "The servants admitted it themselves. Brother Magnus 'employed' them, that was the word they used."

"I've seen no coins anywhere," the prior muttered. "Although I suppose he might have some hidden away. Haltemprice has many dark places that could be used to hide things."

"What are we going to do now?" Tuck asked, staring into the fire gloomily.

"We must send for the coroner," Prior Engayne sighed. "But I feel like we should play down the deaths of the servants, if possible. I'd rather not scare the monks any more than they already are."

"Lock the bodies in the room they're in for now," Will suggested. "The cold should stop them from…you know. At least until the bailiff and coroner can arrive."

The prior dropped his head and ran a hand across his face, plainly exhausted. "You know what those people are like, brother," he muttered. "It might be days – weeks! – before they turn up."

"We'll deal with it," Tuck said to him kindly. "I know this is all a great shock for you, Father."

"Thank you, Brother Tuck," the elderly man said with just a hint of a smile.

"I'd suggest confining Edward Magnus to his cell, if he has one," John said. "Or some other room if not. One we can lock, that he can't escape from."

"I can't do that," the prior replied, spreading his hands wide apologetically. "Brother Magnus came to us on the recommendation of John de Egglescliffe, Bishop of Llandaff."

"Who's he?" Will asked.

"Very powerful Augustinian," Tuck replied.

"Exactly," said the prior. "I'm not sure of their connection, but the bishop spoke very highly of Brother Magnus and I got the impression they are friends, or perhaps even kin. Like I said before, until we have proof that the cellarer has done something criminal, I cannot punish him, or imprison him."

"Then what do we do?" Will demanded, his temper beginning to get the better of him.

"We can at least question him?" John asked the prior.

"Of course."

"Then that's what we do now," the bailiff decided, getting to his feet and rubbing his neck which had grown stiff. None of them were as young as they'd once been and the weather and sinister atmosphere in the priory was not doing John any favours. "We've been sidetracked every time we've tried so far. No more. Let's find this cellarer, and finally hear what he has to say for himself."

NINETEEN

John had no idea what to expect when they strode through the corridors on the way to find Brother Edward Magnus. Although they were slowly growing more familiar with the priory there were areas, and passageways, that they had never been in yet so Prior Engayne had summoned someone to help them move around.

"Simon!" Tuck smiled as he saw his friend coming to escort them through the building. "I've hardly seen you since, well, in a while." He trailed off, clearly not wishing to remind the cantor of their experience on the hilltop.

"I heard you almost succumbed to the cold out there this morning," de Poher said, a worried frown on his gaunt face. "Are you well, brother?"

"Quite well," Tuck assured him before introducing him to Will and John.

Little John was not impressed by the man, whose darting eyes and fidgeting hands told of a nervous disposition that was surely not being helped by living at Haltemprice Priory. Still, there was no sign of duplicity or dishonesty in the monk and they followed him gladly enough through the cloisters towards the refectory.

"I believe we may find Brother Magnus in here, as it's time for the afternoon meal."

"How many meals a day do you have?" Will asked.

De Poher looked at him a little sheepishly. "Well, officially, we only really have one main meal, at midday," he said. "But sometimes we'll have another one. Or two." He turned away and hurried along, sandals slapping on the stone floor. The snow had stopped and sunshine was beginning to melt the worst of it while the wind had died down to the merest whisper through the shuttered windows of the cloisters.

Brother de Poher led them into the refectory where some of the monks were indeed eating a meal. John noticed that they ate no meat, but their plates were piled high with bread and vegetables, and they had wine to drink. No one spoke and the bailiff was surprised to see the monks communicating with a sort of sign language. It was a strange, solemn scene, and it only added to the otherworldliness of the priory in general.

Tuck was the first to notice Brother Magnus, sipping from a cup of wine which he held in both hands as seemed to be the custom in the refectory. The friar gave Simon de Poher's arm a nudge and nodded his head in the cellarer's direction.

Wordlessly, de Poher held up a finger for the three visitors to wait and he went to whisper in Brother Magnus's ear. The cellarer gazed at John and his companions with the hint of a mocking smile tugging at his mouth, but he murmured something to de Poher and got to his feet. Silently, Magnus glided past them and de Poher followed with John and his friends coming after them.

Still nothing was said as Magnus led them unhurriedly around the cloisters and into a room that the guests had not been in before.

"This is the chapter house," de Poher said quietly as he ushered them inside. "We use this chamber for meetings." He smiled. "It's cosier than most places within the priory grounds."

There was a fire burning low in the hearth and Edward Magnus moved to it, placing a small log into the ashes and using a poker to stir the flames to life. De Poher gestured to a bench, bidding the others to sit, but neither John nor Will did so. The sight of the tall cellarer holding a possible weapon was enough to make them wary.

Soon, the fire was blazing merrily and the atmosphere in the room was surprisingly pleasant.

"Gentlemen," said Brother Magnus, sitting on a stone bench adjacent to the hearth, his disrespectful smile growing wider as he addressed them. "What can I do for you?"

John examined the cellarer, taking the man's measure. Not a great deal shorter than the massive bailiff, Edward Magnus was striking, thanks in part to the grey moustache and beard he affected. Even John knew that monks were supposed to be clean shaven, yet there sat the cellarer with neat, grey facial hair that gave him a distinctly goatish appearance. He even seemed to have two cowlicks at the front of his tonsure which resembled horns.

It was almost too ludicrous to take in and John wondered if the cellarer actually cultivated his appearance to give himself a devilish air. The bailiff was forced to admit, much to his distaste, that, while

Edward Magnus should have appeared comical, the man's bullish self-confidence gave him a distinctly impressive demeanour.

"Where were you last night?" Will asked the man without preamble.

"I beg your pardon?" Magnus returned, smirk still in place. "Who the devil are you?"

"This is Will Scaflock," said Simon de Poher. "Forgive me, Edward, for not making introductions. This," he gestured at the bailiff next. "This is John Little. And you've met Brother Tuck."

"Yes, I have indeed met the friar before," Magnus drawled, his eyes seeming to dismiss Tuck as hardly worth his time. "And I've heard of the other two. Who hasn't heard of the infamous, vicious outlaws." He gave an exaggerated shudder and shrank back against the wall as though frightened.

"Where were you last night?" Will repeated, masterfully holding his anger in check.

"Answer him," John added firmly. "I'm a bailiff, and we're here to investigate some very serious crimes. If you want to clear your name, you'd do well to work with us, brother, not against us."

"Your question is ridiculous," the cellarer replied, leaning forward and speaking in harsh, clipped tones. "Where do you think I was last night? I was here, asleep in the dormitory until the crack of dawn, when I rose with my brothers to attend Prime."

"Prime?" John asked, turning to Will and Tuck.

"The first mass of the day," said Scarlet.

"And the other monks saw you there?" John asked. "What about during the night?"

"Well, it's bloody dark inside the dormitory!" retorted the cellarer. "I have no idea if anyone saw me or not, but whatever you're accusing me of, I'm damn sure no one saw me doing that."

His arrogance emanated from him in an unpleasant wave that made John's skin crawl and he would have liked to grab the goat-like man by the neck and force the truth from him. Such behaviour would never be tolerated in the priory, however, and he pushed down his anger.

"What did you discover when you visited the site of the pigs' sacrifice?" Tuck asked.

"They had been ritually slaughtered," replied the cellarer matter-of-factly. "A sacrifice to Lucifer."

Tuck frowned, clearly taken aback. "How do you know that?" he asked.

"Just certain signs," Magnus replied smoothly. "I am an expert in these matters, as you know."

"I'll bet you bloody are," Will Scarlet growled, eliciting another mocking smile from the cellarer.

"What about the grave that was opened and robbed last night?" John asked, folding his arms across his great barrel chest.

"What of it?"

"What did you make of it when you heard the news?"

"I have not seen the burial ground since it was" – Magnus paused and then, with a little snort that might have been disgust but might just as easily have been amusement or even titillation – "desecrated. So I can make no real judgement of the perpetrator's purpose."

"Take a guess," Tuck said. "Since you are an expert on these occult matters."

The cellarer nodded sagely. "A guess? I would say the bones were stolen to be used in some ritual, most likely as an offering to Belial."

"Belial?" John sucked a breath through his teeth and looked at his friends in amazement. "Lucifer? Belial? What are we dealing with here, Tuck? This is all way above my head. What next?"

"Next?" Brother Magnus repeated, tilting his head to the side thoughtfully. "Next I would imagine there will be a sacrifice to Leviathan."

"And what would be a suitable sacrifice to Leviathan?" Friar Tuck asked, making the sign of the cross as he spoke.

"Who can say? Perhaps the murder of a man. Maybe even of more than one man."

"Three men?" Will demanded.

"That would be suitable, yes," the cellarer said, staring unblinkingly at Scarlet.

"You know three of your servants were murdered earlier today?" John asked, watching the goatish occultist for his reaction.

Magnus merely nodded slowly. "Oh no, that is horrific," he said, in a voice that suggested he did not really think it that horrific at all. "But it doesn't surprise me."

"Really?" laughed Tuck, astonished. "Why not? I'd have thought the murder of three men within a priory would be terrible shock to any sane person."

"Maybe so," Magnus returned coolly. "But it does not surprise me. In fact, I expected something like this. You see," he rose up and held his hands out to the hearth, warming his long, delicate fingers. "Whoever is behind all this has a plan." He stood with his back to them, warmed by the flames which John imagined were almost licking out like fiery, hellish fingers, reaching to stroke Edward Magnus.

John sniffed and shared a glance with his companions – there was the smell again, and it was strong and repulsive and clearly emanating from the man by the hearth.

"A plan?" asked Tuck. "Can you foresee what might come next in this madman's plan?"

Brother Magnus turned back to them, the flickering firelight making strange shadows dance across his bearded face as he smiled broadly. "I foresee," he said, "another blood sacrifice. What form it might take, I cannot say for sure, but I know who it will be dedicated to."

John swallowed, unnerved by the cellarer's performance, and apparent enjoyment of the situation. "Who will it be dedicated to?" he asked softly, wondering if he really wanted to know the answer.

"Isn't it obvious?" Magnus retorted. "What about you, Brother Tuck? Can you not guess? If we assume dark deeds have been carried out in praise of Lucifer, Belial, and Leviathan, who might the fourth, and greatest ceremony be dedicated to?"

John looked at his portly friend and saw the blood drain from his face.

"The fourth crown prince of Hell," murmured the friar, drawing out his rosary beads, fingers working nervously along them as he stared at the smiling cellarer and finished in a guttural tone that seemed almost to be dragged from his unwilling throat, "Satan himself."

TWENTY

"This is insane," Will Scarlet hissed when the three friends sat alone in the chapter house, shivering in spite of the fire. "Absolutely insane. We're not qualified to deal with this kind of thing. I don't even know why we're here. This is a job for priests and bishops. Pope John, even!"

Brothers Magnus and de Poher had left the chamber to be about their business, the former apparently excited by his dire prediction, the latter as anxious and frightened as ever.

"D'you think he speaks the truth?" John asked, biting his lower lip as he stood and looked out at the snow-covered ground. "All that about crown princes of Hell, and Belial and..." He trailed off and waved a hand uncomfortably.

Tuck made a dismissive sound and came to stand beside the huge bailiff, patting him on the back as though John was a frightened child. "Forget about Belial and Satan," he said. "We are in a house of God, surrounded by monks. I'm a friar myself." He held up his pectoral cross, its wood worn smooth over years and thousands of prayers. "I wouldn't be worried about supernatural forces here in Haltemprice Priory."

"It's easy to say that," said Will, coming to rub his hands before the hearth. "But we've all felt that oppressive atmosphere about the place since we got here. We're not imagining it, Tuck, and it's not normal!"

The friar didn't reply to that. There was certainly something to Will's words, he had to admit. "If we can prove Edward Magnus is guilty of the three murders, or any of the other crimes, he'll be arrested and the pall that hangs over these lands will fade. Focus on that, my friends, not thoughts of demons. The only demon we need to worry about is the damned cellarer."

"But what about all that he was saying?" John persisted. "I'll fight any man, you know that, Tuck. But Leviathan? Lucifer? How can we fight them? What weapons do we have to fight the likes of them?"

"He's just made all that up," Tuck replied, shaking his head in disgust. "Oh, don't get me wrong, I believe in demons – in Satan – like we all do. But what Magnus was saying was all just bluster to frighten superstitious folks. He's read about the crown princes of Hell in one of those blasphemous tomes he keeps in his library and thought it would be a good way to dissuade people from looking at his work too closely." He patted John on the back again, a twinkle in his eye. "You'll be fine, boys. I'm here!"

Will Scarlet was clearly not convinced. He did smile though as he asked, "What about the rituals Brother Magnus mentioned? There have been three so far."

"Rituals? Pfft." Tuck rolled his eyes in disgust. "There has been one – one! – that we know of: the pigs that were sacrificed. But we have no idea what the Anglo-Saxon grave was opened for, or what was done with the stolen bones. And as for the three servants in the undercroft? They were murdered, plain and simple, so that they couldn't testify against Edward Magnus."

"But how?" John demanded. "How did he manage it with us in the undercroft at the same time?"

The friar gave a shrug as if that question was unimportant. "He can move very quietly, as I know from personal experience, and those three men were bound and gagged," he reminded his friends. "Utterly at their murderer's mercy. That was no black magic ritual, just a cowardly attack on defenceless men."

"No ritual?" John asked, coming away from the window to stand beside Will at the hearth. "How d'you know that?"

"Did you see any of the things normally associated with a ritual?" Tuck returned, pouring some wine from a jug on a table set against the wall. "Candles? Books? Incense? Think of Mass as a ritual, John. Was there anything at all like that in the undercroft when we found the bodies?"

"Well, no," the bailiff admitted. "But maybe this kind of black ceremony doesn't need all that stuff. Maybe Edward Magnus is so skilled that he can contact the crown princes of Hell without candles and bells and all that carry on."

"He has a point," Will added. "If I say a prayer in my own house, am I wasting my time? Does there need to be candles and incense to speak to God?" He thought for a moment and then finished, "Or demons, in this case."

Tuck looked at them as if they'd just uttered some terrible blasphemy themselves and then he raised his hands and looked around him. "How can you ask something like that within these walls? Of course ritual matters. You can say a prayer on your own, but that will obviously not be as potent as saying a prayer in a house of God, alongside a hundred monks, with candles, incense and all the paraphernalia that makes a Mass so powerful."

John made a noncommittal sound, apparently not convinced by his friend's argument.

"Think about it," Tuck continued more forcefully. "Just killing three men isn't a ritual, is it?"

"It might be," Will said. "If the killer said some prayers to demons when he was going about his work."

"It really doesn't matter either way," the friar sighed. "Ritual or not, Edward Magnus has specifically warned us another crime has yet to be committed. A fourth abomination. We must stop him."

"Bit hard, when the prior won't let us lock the bastard away."

"He will, John," said Tuck. "Once we prove that Magnus was involved in the crimes."

"How?" Will asked.

"We should check the undercroft again," suggested the friar. "I believe that's the epicentre of all the evil that surrounds Haltemprice. Let's go down there and search it thoroughly. There must be something that'll help us prove Brother Magnus's guilt."

"What if he's down there and tries to stop us?" John wondered.

"Let him try," said Will, leading the way out the door, fists clenched and in no mood to be put off his task.

TWENTY-ONE

The three friends walked with purpose, grim-faced, stoic, and ready to discover what they could in the draughty undercroft.

That was what Tuck had decided to focus upon as they each found a candle and lit it in the cloisters. The air remained utterly frigid, and the sense of impending doom still lay across the priory, but at least the storm had abated and the candles merely flickered rather than blowing out immediately as they opened the undercroft door and descended the stairs again.

It was an unsettling feeling as they moved along the passageway knowing three men had recently been slaughtered within one of the side rooms, their corpses still lying there uninterred.

Most undercrofts that Tuck had ever seen were fairly open affairs, but this one had wooden walls added to create smaller chambers that could be closed off, and the friar found himself dearly wishing it was not so. It made the whole place hideously claustrophobic and Tuck held his breath as Will opened the door that separated them from the dead men.

What if the bodies were gone? Thoughts of the servants, somehow reanimated by Brother Magnus's occult powers, filled Tuck's mind and he swallowed, knowing he was being foolish. Still, he couldn't help but heave a sigh of relief as he saw the corpses lying where they'd been left.

"We can't just leave them like that until the coroner turns up," John muttered. "It's cold down here, but they'll still rot. Besides," he looked at the friar, "they should be given a Christian burial, should they not? This seems, I don't know, sacrilegious or something."

"I suppose so," Tuck murmured. "Prior Engayne will have been in shock when he agreed to leave them here. We'll speak with him when we're finished."

John led the way back into the passageway and hissed, staring at the flame of his candle. "Look," he said. "It's flickering."

"There's a draught again," Will noted, shivering as an icy blast of wind blew through the undercroft and he cupped a hand around his own candle so it wouldn't go out.

"It makes no sense," John said, still in a whisper as his eyes searched the shadows nervously. "Where is it coming from?"

"It's stopped now," Tuck noted, eyeing his candle whose flame stood tall and straight again. "Come on."

He led the way to the chamber at the end where Edward Magnus liked to work. The door was closed but the three men didn't hesitate, lifting the latch and walking inside. They were ready for another fight and, in truth, would probably welcome the chance to let out some of their pent-up frustration, but the room was empty.

"Smell that?"

"Aye, John," Tuck agreed, sniffing the air distastefully. "Brother Magnus has been down here."

"Where the hell is he now then?" Will demanded, searching the room just as they'd done before and, as before, seeing no sign of the cellarer anywhere. The strange smell was strong though, and suggested Edward Magnus had been there mere moments before.

Friar Tuck stood for a breathless second gazing around the chamber, and then something seemed to tickle his memory and he struggled to grasp hold of it before it faded. "Wait," he said excitedly. "I've seen this room before. The nightmares I was suffering the first few days I was here." He walked towards the far wall and the bookcase that stood there. "This," he said. "I remember this!"

Will and John watched their friend in silence as he stooped and held his candle near the floor.

"Look!" the friar said in triumph, and then he straightened and reached out to the bookcase, dragging it forward. His companions gasped as the heavy piece of furniture, stacked with great tomes, easily slid away from the wall.

"How did you do that?" John demanded.

"It's hinged," Tuck replied, examining the left-hand side of the bookcase. "And it must be cleverly weighted, with ball-bearings attached underneath. Look." He gestured at the floor which bore light scrape marks.

"Never mind that," said Will, looking past the shifted bookcase and staring at the wall. "Look there. That must be where the draught keeps coming from."

They all saw it then: a door, big enough for a man to fit through, hidden whenever the bookcase was in place.

"Where does it go?" John asked Tuck fearfully. "Did you see that in your nightmares?"

Tuck shook his head and took out his trusty cudgel. "If I did, I don't remember, but I'm ready to find out. Are you?" He peered uncertainly at John and Will and both men nodded, drawing their swords. Afraid of what they might find on the other side of the hidden doorway, but determined to see things through to the end.

"Lead on then, Tuck," Will Scarlet growled.

"Me?" the friar demanded, not quite so sure of himself as his friend reached out and drew the door open, revealing a gaping black tunnel that led to God knew where.

"Aye, you," John grinned, holding out his sword towards the secret passage. "You promised to look after us, didn't you? Well, say a prayer, old friend, and lead us on, into Hell itself if that's where this leads!"

TWENTY-TWO

The air was mercifully still within the passageway as the three men made their way inside, their candles guttering but not going out. The door did not have a lock on it and, in fact, could be attached to the bookcase so they could both be pulled back into place from within the tunnel, ingeniously hiding things from prying eyes. Little John muttered irritably as they started to move ahead since the tunnel was not large and it was a tight squeeze for the enormous bailiff who was forced to bend uncomfortably as he walked.

"This is incredible," Will murmured, running a hand along the wall that must have been carved from the living rock. "How did it get here?"

"Who knows," said Tuck. "It seems very old, though." He peered at the tunnel walls. "Looks like it was probably dug out many years ago. Perhaps centuries ago."

"So it was already here when the priory was built over it," Will noted. "How did Magnus find it?"

Tuck shook his head. "No idea. Maybe one of his books mentioned it. But that door wasn't as good quality as the others in the priory. I doubt the builders put it in. Perhaps Brother Magnus simply found the tunnel by accident and had his servants put the door there."

"It must lead outside," John grunted, rubbing his head where it had scraped the roof of the cramped passageway. "That's why there's a through-draught every so often."

"That would explain how Magnus was able to kill the three servants," Will noted excitedly. "He was in that room of his when we were fighting with them, and sneaked out through here when he heard what was happening. Wherever this leads to, he was able to work his way back around, into the priory and down into the undercroft where he found his servants, completely at his mercy."

"He stabbed them while we were searching his room," John agreed bitterly. "And then simply walked back up the stairs to the cloisters."

Will was at the front of the slow-moving group and his foot crunched on something. It made an odd, brittle sound and he halted, Tuck and John almost walking into one another.

"What are you doing?" John hissed, claustrophobic within the tight confines of the gloomy, centuried passageway.

"I trod on something," Will replied, holding his candle down to the ground. He looked at the pale, white object and a frown deepened on his face before he turned and eyed his friends pensively. "It's a bone," he told them. "Looks like a human leg bone. And it's been chewed."

"Chewed?" John demanded. "You mean by a person?"

"No. Rats," Will said.

The sudden thought of dozens of scurrying, biting, tearing rats filling the narrow tunnel was not a pleasant one and Tuck gave Scarlet a shove. "Hurry up then," the friar grunted. "Before there's another gust and our candles go out."

That was an even more disturbing idea and Will began moving again, faster now. It was one thing to face a man, or even dozens of men, on a battlefield, quite another to be trapped in a pitch-black tunnel with hundreds of rats swarming over you.

"There," Will murmured after what seemed like hours of walking but was probably only a few heartbeats. "A light ahead."

"Daylight?" John asked, voice filled with hope.

"No," Tuck said, peering over Will's shoulder as the passageway began to widen. "Too yellow. Candles I'd say."

"Then I reckon we've found Brother Magnus," John growled in the familiar tone that Tuck recognised as a precursor to violence. "Be ready, for he may have more of his lackeys with him."

"Lackeys are better than rats," Will said with a portentous laugh as he drew out his sword and led them into an open chamber.

There were no servants inside, but the great room they'd stepped into was incredible. The ceiling was so high above them that their candles' light did not reach it and, from the fetid, damp odour it seemed clear they were deep underground.

It was not entirely dark for, a way ahead, more candles had been lit and set around the top of a circular area about fifteen feet across, and dug five or six feet deeper than the rest of the chamber's floor. From down there, a voice could be heard, speaking in low but excited or perhaps angry tones.

No, Tuck realised, there was more than one voice.

"Two of them," Will whispered, holding up his fingers in case his friends didn't hear him. "At least."

The three placed their candles back in the tunnel so the light wouldn't give them away and then they crept ahead to listen to the voices which were strangely indistinct and difficult to understand.

Tuck's eyes roved around the shadowy edges of the huge chamber, forcing his imagination not to get carried away and tell him there were dozens of pairs of eyes watching them. It was true that things were reflecting Brother Magnus's candlelight, but they were not eyes, Tuck reassured himself. Old coins, perhaps, or maybe even gemstones – who knew what this great old vault had once been used for? Storage for some ancient, wealthy family perhaps. Edward Magnus must be getting money from somewhere after all, or how else was he hiring servants as his personal bodyguards? Those occult books of his would not be cheap either, Tuck was certain of that. Any book was valuable, but rare magical grimoires must be well above what a simple monk could afford.

Then the friar realised what the sparkling things were lying in and upon, and he swallowed, mouth suddenly dry.

"Christ above," Will Scarlet whispered and Tuck knew his friend had also noticed.

"Is that more bones?" John asked, squinting in the direction his companions were looking.

"It's a great bloody mountain of bones," Will gasped. "There must be dozens of them. Hundreds! What the hell have we stumbled into here? What is this place?"

"Another ancient burial site," Tuck guessed. "It seems Edward Magnus is attracted to such ill-omened places. Quiet, though, let's try to hear what he's saying."

Whoever the cellarer was talking to had raised their voice in anger and the three men in the shadows strained to make out the words. The voice was loud, but it had a weird quality to it – unnaturally thin, as if it emanated not from a human throat, but from something much less substantial, like a wraith.

The thought was out before Tuck could suppress it and he shuddered inwardly. Rats, mountains of bones, murders, ritual sacrifices, and now a wraith? God protect them, they should have stayed in bloody Wakefield!

Tuck fully believed in the malevolent powers of Satan — what man of God did not, after all? But the friar was not so convinced in the reality of wraiths and he forced himself to put aside such fears and creep forward, hoping to hear better what was being said and perhaps catch a glimpse of Brother Magnus's companion.

John and Will followed behind him, all three moving with exaggerated care, fearful of standing on another of the scattered, hateful bones and giving themselves away.

"You were warned," the thin, reedy voice was saying. "What you seek requires four rituals. Calling me up was the third, but you cannot avoid the last of them, as fearful as it may seem to you."

"Pah." That was Edward Magnus, his own voice seeming strident and somehow more vital than the other's. "I'm not afraid, I am simply making my preparations."

"Then you had best complete them soon," came the second voice again, and it sounded pleased, as though the speaker was amused by Magnus's troubles. "Or the law will put an end to your work, brother, and calling me up for advice will have been for naught."

Edward Magnus remained silent at that, as though he'd taken on board the other's criticism. "Fear not, Ecgbert," he replied after a long moment. "See, your bones have all been consumed. No other shall ever call you forth again. And my work here is almost complete – soon enough the pall that hangs over the priory will fade, and I will move on to continue my work elsewhere."

Tuck's eyes widened as he listened. 'Ecgbert'? Wasn't that the name of the old Anglo-Saxon sorcerer whose grave had been emptied and whose sword they'd found? Was Edward Magnus somehow conversing with a man who'd lain dead and buried for centuries? It seemed incredible. Impossible!

"Move on as soon as you can," the shrill, piping voice came again. "From what you tell me, you've already drawn too much attention to yourself."

"It will have been worth it though," Brother Magnus replied. "For I shall live on, younger than now."

"Come on," murmured John. "I've heard enough of this insanity. We move now before we lose our chance and these bastards somehow escape." He stood up, followed by Will and finally Tuck, all three holding their weapons as they strode towards the circle of candles that contained their quarry.

The bailiff's massive foot crushed another ancient bone into fragments, the resulting crack echoing back from the benighted walls and Tuck saw Edward Magnus turn to face them, surprise and rage etched on his goatish features.

"You're under arrest," Little John called out, and his rich baritone was a grating contrast to the thin voice of Ecgbert. "You can come with me peacefully, or you can fight us. Personally, I hope you choose to fight."

It was only then that Tuck noticed there was only one person within the circle of candles. Brother Magnus was alone.

The friar hurried ahead, grey robe flapping about his ankles as he looked all around and into the deep shadows for some sign of whoever the cellarer had been conversing with. There was no one, yet there had been no time for the second man to have run away!

"Who were you talking to?" John demanded as he drew nearer to Edward Magnus. "Where is he?"

"Your puny mind couldn't comprehend even if I told you," the cellarer replied acidly, and turned to run in the opposite direction.

"Catch him!" Tuck shouted unnecessarily for his friends were already going after the fugitive. "Hurry!"

"We're going as fast we can," Will Scarlet retorted, red-faced and gesturing downwards with his sword. Beneath them were more bones, forming a blanket in this area that must have been a handspan deep. It was impossible to move quickly on such a hideous, shifting floor, and soon Edward Magnus had reached an archway that marked the entrance to a flight of ancient stone steps.

With a last, sneering look over his shoulder, the cellarer began his ascent, disappearing from view.

"He's getting away," John shouted.

"What about the man he was talking to?" Will called back, cursing as he skidded and fell painfully amongst the scattered remnants of aeons-old human remains.

"Disappeared into thin air," Tuck told him. "But never mind that. We need to get to those stairs. They must lead out of here, and if Magnus reaches a door that to the outside, the candles—"

He broke off as the metallic clatter of a heavy door opening filtered down to them and then came the gust of air the friar had been dreading and every candle in the underground chamber was extinguished, plunging the three friends into total, impenetrable darkness.

TWENTY-THREE

"Stay where you are!" Tuck cried, his words reverberating around the great, black chamber.

"What are we going to do?" Will demanded, voice betraying the terror that was rising within him. "I can't see a thing!"

Above them, Edward Magnus slammed the door he'd escaped through and the sound of heavy bolts being slipped into place told the three friends that they would not be leaving that horrific charnel house in the same direction.

"Stay calm," Tuck soothed, although he felt fear stealing his breath even as he did his best to reassure his friends. It wasn't so much the dark – it was the thought of being surrounded by the remains of so many dead people, and the rats that gnawed on their pale, discarded bones. The friar grasped his cross and began to recite the Pater Noster, trying to draw courage from the familiar prayer.

A grating sound came to them, and then a rattle as bones shifted.

"What was that?" Will shouted.

"It was me," John called back, and he sounded just as frightened as the other two.

Would they be lost down there? Tuck wondered. Was that what had happened to all the others whose scattered bodies lay strewn about the place? Would Edward Magnus hurry back around to the cloisters and down into the undercroft where he could seal up the door to the tunnel that had brought Tuck and his companions into this horrific vault of the dead?

Panic rose in the friar again, and the sound of tiny, skittering feet away to his left made his heart pound in his chest. There were rats in there with them he knew, perhaps hundreds of them, and they would be hungry for the taste of human flesh! Their sharp little teeth, rending and tearing, claws scratching for purchase on his pale skin…

"This is bloody stupid," John burst out, and then the sound of bones being scattered hither and thither filled the air.

"What are you doing?" Will demanded.

"I'm going to find the wall," John replied breathlessly. "And then work my way around until I find the tunnel we came through. The candles are there."

"Good idea!" Will shouted, hope replacing the panic Tuck had heard in his voice before. "Let's all do the same."

The thought of forcing his way blindly through so many human bones made the friar's stomach churn, but he knew he would die if he did not get the hell out of that chamber. He started to walk as best he could, praying to God and every saint he could think of that he was moving in the right direction.

"God, I hear the rats," Will cried, and his voice was the closest Tuck had ever heard it come to a whimper.

"They won't bother us," John replied firmly. "Just take care not to trip on all these old bones. I don't want to have to haul one of you two through that tunnel if you break a leg."

Tuck held his hands out before him, stepping as carefully as possible as he prayed he'd find the wall.

The darkness was so complete that he almost felt like he was trapped within a cocoon. Or a grave.

He stopped moving and grasped his cross, the old, familiar wood reassuring him and calming his laboured breaths. He would survive this. He'd survived his ordeal in the snow hadn't he? God was with him, as He always was. With that thought bringing him courage, Tuck began to recite some of Psalm 23, feeling it appropriate for the dire predicament they were in.

"The Lord is my shepherd; I shall not want.
He maketh me to lie down in green pastures: he leadeth me beside the still waters.
He restoreth my soul: he leadeth me in the paths of righteousness for his name's sake.
Yea, though I walk through the valley of the shadow of death, I will fear no evil: for thou art with me; thy rod and thy staff they comfort me."

Tuck finished with that line and, as he fell silent John and Will joined in fervent 'Amens'.

Nodding in satisfaction, the friar put one foot in front of the other again, stepping gingerly, making sure his footing was secure before placing his full weight down. The darkness was such a contrast to the snow, he thought, yet so similar in some ways. One was white, one was black, but both were blinding, and both did strange things to the mind, making one think he was going insane after a time.

"I'm at the wall!" John called out, plainly elated, and then Tuck felt his fingers strike something cold and hard and he knew he too had reached the edge of the great chamber.

Soon Will had also informed them he'd found the wall and then Tuck almost began crying with relief as he saw a spark nearby, the tiny sliver of light only lasting for a moment but it was enough to show John's calm, stern face.

"Good job," Will Scarlet said, beaming in relief as John's tinder caught light and he brought life to the first of their candles. "Now we just need to hope that bastard cellarer doesn't open another door and blow them out again!"

"We know where we are now," John replied, a huge grin peeking out from his grizzled beard. "We just need to follow the tunnel back to the undercroft, and then Brother Magnus will get what's coming to him."

All three candles were quickly lit and the friends began the claustrophobic journey back along the narrow passageway, hope making their steps lighter than Tuck would have thought possible when they'd first been trapped in the horrible charnel pit.

"Who was Magnus talking to?" John wondered as he forced his massive shoulders through a tight section of the tunnel. "That's what gets me the most. There was no one else there!"

"He must have been talking to himself," Tuck said, trying to convince himself as much as his companions. "We've all seen that kind of madness before. Brother Magnus is clearly moon-touched. Having a conversation with himself is the least of his unusual habits."

"That wasn't his voice," Will muttered, but he did not elaborate and neither did the other two. They might be out of the darkness, but none of them would feel safe until they were back standing in the open air, even if it was snowing or blowing a gale outside.

"How are we going to prove all this?" Tuck asked as they walked. "We still only have vague theories. We don't even have a motive for Brother Magnus's actions."

"A motive?" Will returned venomously. "He's bloody mad! That's his motive."

"Maybe. But the coroner will need more than that to convict him, especially if he's really a friend of Bishop de Egglescliffe as the prior suggested."

"What about Ecgbert?" John said as they came at last to the end of the tunnel. "That's who he was talking to wasn't it?"

"It's who he thought he was talking to," Tuck said. "But please, John, get that door open before I suffocate in here!"

John did not hesitate. He did not even attempt to find the latch, he leaned back and lifted his leg, the great thigh muscles bulging as he slammed his boot into the wood and it splintered with a terrific crack.

They re-entered the cellarer's work room, drawing their weapons once more in case the madman was there waiting for them, but the chamber was empty.

"Come on," Will Scarlet ordered, not waiting around. "Let's get the hell back up to the cloisters. If I never have to come into a cellar or an undercroft again it'll be too damn soon!"

TWENTY-FOUR

It was not snowing when the three companions burst into the cloisters and threw open the door that led out to the herb garden. The sky was heavy and thick with dark grey clouds and there was a whistling wind that cut right to the bone, but Tuck and his friends did not care. They stood, looking at one another and up at the sky, breathing in the air and thanking God for delivering them from the priory's awful underbelly.

"Will the sun ever shine on this place again?" Will asked, shaking his head and clearing snow from a bench with his arm before sitting on it and sighing in sheer exhaustion.

"Of course it will," said Tuck. "Evil may hold sway over Haltemprice for now, but God will prevail, as we have."

"We're not done yet," John noted, resting his palm on the pommel of his sword. "We need to find the cellarer so, on your feet Will. Not a moment to waste."

"He'll be long gone."

"Probably," John agreed. "Or he'll be sitting somewhere acting all innocent. Either way, we need to find him and see what he has to say for himself. There must be some evidence around here that ties him to the crimes."

Some of the monks were working in the cloisters again now that the storm had passed. Tuck called one over and asked him to find Prior Engayne. While they waited they questioned the other monks, asking if any had seen Brother Magnus in the past hour or so. None had.

"What's been happening now?" The prior appeared from the direction of the chapter house looking as tired as Tuck felt. "Did you find anything?"

"Aye," John told him, nodding. "Did you know there's a tunnel in the undercroft that leads to a great chamber filled with human bones?"

The prior simply stared up at him for a long moment, and then his mouth worked but no sound came out until, at last, he managed to say, "What?"

"In the room the cellarer uses for his studies," John told him. "There's a tunnel hidden behind the bookcase."

"This is the first I've ever heard of it," the prior admitted, a stunned look on his face. "And it leads to…" He trailed off, shaking his head. "How do you know all this?"

"The draught," said Will. "We knew it had to be coming through the cellar from somewhere, and Tuck discovered a door behind the bookcase. We went through it, along an ancient passageway, and found ourselves in an enormous room where Brother Magnus was, well, we're not sure exactly what he was doing, but he ran off when he saw us and locked us in. We might have died down there!"

It was all too much for Prior Engayne to take in at once and he sat on the bench Will had occupied earlier, not even bothering to clear the snow.

"There's a flight of steps at the opposite end of that underground vault," Tuck said. "That's how Magnus escaped from us. But they must lead to a door somewhere near here on the surface." He held his arm up and pointed to the north. "Maybe, what?" He turned to John and Will. "Half a mile from here?"

"Nah, not that far," the bailiff said. "It felt like that when we were down there walking, but I'd say it was no more than a quarter of a mile from the undercroft to the chamber of bones."

"The Chamber of Bones," Prior Engayne breathed, pronouncing it as if it were an official title. Which it probably would be now, for it was such a fitting name for the place.

"Are there any buildings you know of to the north that could lead down into a huge hidden vault, Father?" Tuck asked.

"I can't think," the prior admitted, closing his eyes and dipping his head. "Maybe. There are some storehouses out in that direction."

Tuck called to a monk who was busy at a writing desk a short distance along the cloister from them. "The prior is very tired," he told the man, who looked middle-aged and competent. "Take care of him please, brother."

"I will pass the word around," Prior Engayne called after them as they headed towards the doors that would take them to the main courtyard. "If Brother Magnus shows up, I'll have him locked away until we can find out what's happening here. I'll also place guards on the door to the undercroft!"

The three companions went outside and began walking northwards through the snow. There was little to break up the whiteness of the surrounding lands other than a robin with its red breast flitting about nearby, but the storehouses the prior had told them about were easily visible.

"Two of them," Will grunted as he forced his way through the deep snow. "Which one should we head for first?"

"The one with footprints leading from it," Tuck replied, and they trudged on, heading for the westernmost building until they could see the blanket of snow around its entrance remained pure and untouched after the storm.

"Weapons at the ready," John warned as they changed course and neared the other storehouse.

"What for?" Will asked. "Look, there's his footprints leading away. He's not inside."

"Better safe than sorry," the bailiff replied and tried the ill-fitting but thick door. It was locked but the pair of bolts holding it in place opened easily.

The meagre daylight was just enough to let them see inside and it was immediately obvious where the entrance to the underground chamber was hidden for there was a pile of earth in the corner revealing a thick iron trapdoor. It took only a moment for John and Will to lift the trapdoor which opened easily.

Sticking his head into the hole, Tuck could see another passageway leading off a short distance towards a dark void that he guessed must be the steps down to the charnel house.

"This is it," he said, grunting as he pulled himself back to his feet and looked around. The storehouse was a single-storey building of stone construction and it, or its predecessors, had probably stood there for hundreds of years before the new priory was built and it had then been turned into this place for gardening equipment and other tools. "Somehow Brother Magnus knew of the location of this trapdoor," the friar mused. "And he came here and dug it up, keeping it hidden with a thin layer of earth when he wasn't using it. Today he was in too much of a hurry running from us to bother pushing the earth back into position."

"This is all too incredible," Will Scarlet opined, heading outside and scanning the land hopefully for the cellarer. "How could he have known about this place? And about the tunnel from the undercroft?"

"I have no idea," Tuck admitted.

"Me neither," said John. "Maybe Ecgbert, whoever he is, told Magnus about them. Either way, he's left footprints in the snow. Let's see if we can track the bastard."

It was a simple matter to follow the trail left by the fleeing cellarer for his were the only prints around. Everyone had been sheltering in the priory during the storm and even for a time afterwards, so there was no chance the companions would take a wrong turn or become confused over which direction they should go in next. Where the tracks led to was perhaps no great surprise.

"Oh well," Tuck said when they reached the end of the trail. "We're back where we started. Brother Magnus is somewhere inside Haltemprice Priory."

"Good," Will grunted. "He won't escape again, even if I have to tear this place apart stone by stone!"

TWENTY-FIVE

The three companions strode back into the main priory buildings, grim faced and with their weapons drawn. The monks they passed recognised them so were more curious than alarmed, but none admitted to having seen the wanted cellarer.

"Where to start?" Will wondered, looking around. "This place is pretty big and with all the scaffolding and construction supplies lying around there's plenty of spots for the bastard to hide in."

"We have to hope the snow will keep him here," Tuck said. "No one would attempt to travel through that. Even the horses wouldn't get far with the roads in the state they are. So we simply need to hunt until we find him. Someone must have seen him, surely."

"Maybe we should call the monks together and ask them to raise the alarm if they see him," Will suggested.

"Prior Engayne will have done that already," Tuck said with a shake of his head. "And I'd rather not involve the brothers in this if we can avoid it. Magnus has murdered at least three men already; I'd rather not put more of them at risk. Let's just move through each area methodically until we find him."

"All right then," John said. "Let's get to it then. Who would have keys to all the locked rooms in the priory?"

"The sacrist," Will told him.

"Indeed," Tuck agreed, leading the way to the church.

They found the monk they were looking for in the sacristy and, thankfully, he'd been told of their mission by Prior Engayne so readily handed over a great bunch of keys that would grant them access to everywhere within the main priory buildings.

"Make sure you bring them all safely back to me," the sacrist warned them testily. "Some of them don't have spares."

"We'll take care of them, don't worry, brother," Will told him respectfully. He knew how hard the sacrist's job was, taking care of the very fabric of the church - plate, vestments, shrines, the Eucharist, ornaments, holy oils, relics and so on. "Just you be careful if you see the cellarer. Don't get in his way."

The sacrist was a tall, grim-faced priest, and he nodded seriously at Will. "As long as he doesn't try to interfere with any of my duties, I'll leave him alone."

"Good man," John replied, and the three former outlaws left the church to begin their search.

They moved around the rooms leading off the cloisters first and widened their search as time went on. They walked through the refectory, kitchen, dormitory, latrines, warming house, chapter house, infirmary, chapels, and even the prior's own chambers without discovering their quarry. Monks eyed them with great interest as they went about their business although they had sheathed their weapons by now. Even so, life in a priory was a very routine one and these hard men striding purposefully around the place hunting for one of their own brothers provided some welcome excitement. It lifted the oppressive atmosphere if only for a little while.

It was interesting for Little John too, for he'd never seen inside all the areas of a great building like this before, unlike Tuck and Will. The building was impressive even at this unfinished stage of its construction, and, when the monks began singing in the nearby church at Vespers the chanting seemed to drive away the sense of impending doom for a time.

It did not last long.

"You can't come along here."

Little John halted and his companions followed suit, eyeing the skinny, unkempt fellow with a bulbous nose who'd stepped out of a side room and barred their way. He held a wooden cudgel much like the one Tuck carried but, even so, did not strike them as much of a threat.

"Why not?" John asked, playing along with the man.

"Because only monks are allowed along here."

"Who are you?" Tuck demanded. "We've been granted access to every part of this place by Prior Engayne himself. Look." He rattled the great ring of keys that the sacrist had given them.

"I'm one of the servants," the skinny man snarled. "A guard. I stop people going into areas they shouldn't be in."

"Well, you're not stopping us," Will Scarlet retorted, stepping forward, fists clenched menacingly. "So, either you get out the way, or I'll have to move you."

"You won't enjoy that," John added with a broad grin. "He's not very gentle."

"Neither are we," the servant said, and he was smiling too, revealing a row of blackened teeth that reminded Tuck of tombstones in a graveyard. Another four men appeared then, lining up beside the skinny one and completely blocking the corridor.

"The prior will see you all removed from your positions here," Tuck warned them, doing his best to avoid violence within a house of God, although even his temper was beginning to fray around the edges at this point. These servants had to be acting on Brother Magnus's orders, and that meant they were close to finding him.

"Who cares?" the unkempt servant asked, still smirking. "We've been very, very nicely paid to keep you lads away, and we'll soon find somewhere else to work. Always people looking for good men like us."

Tuck opened his mouth to try and persuade the servants further but Will Scarlet had waited long enough. With a bellow of animal rage, he launched himself at the man on the right of the group.

Tuck's cudgel was out in an instant but the skinny servant was bringing his down towards the friar's head before Tuck could move out of the way. Lifting his arm, he roared in pain as his right bicep took most of the force. Instinct took over and he lashed out, smashing the man in the teeth with his left fist and sending him sprawling backwards, bleeding and stunned.

Will Scarlet had already beaten his opponent, catching him off-guard with a blistering uppercut before kneeing him in the jaw as he fell.

Little John had used his great bulk to pin one of the remaining two men against the wall, but the last of them had struck him a blow with his cudgel and was winding up for a second, directly to the crown of

John's head, when Will Scarlet kicked him right in the spine. The servant's cudgel dropped with a clatter on the floor and the man himself went face-first into the stone wall.

"Hurry up and deal with him," Scarlet shouted at John, who hooked his arm around the final servant's neck and squeezed until the fellow passed out.

"Good," Tuck said, breathing heavily and making the sign of the cross as he eyed their handiwork. "We didn't kill anyone, I don't think, and no blood was spilled within God's house. Well, not that much."

"A few teeth were knocked out," Will chuckled, waving his fist and blowing on it ruefully. "And, oh wait…this one's still awake." The skinny servant who'd initially barred their way was crouched on all fours, pressing a hand to his injured mouth. He turned and glared at Scarlet, threatening to kill him, before the former outlaw's boot cannoned into the side of his head and he fell silently to the floor.

"He's sleeping now," John murmured grimly. "Let's find out what they were trying to stop us from seeing along here."

The room the servants had come from was unoccupied, frustratingly, just a sparsely furnished monk's cell, and the three friends moved on, knowing one of the other chambers further along must finally hold the man they were hunting.

"The sun is setting," Tuck noted. "It'll be dark soon and"— he broke off as the next door along suddenly flew open and a man came reeling out.

"Brother de Poher!" Tuck called, recognising his old friend. "Whatever's the matter?"

De Poher turned to them, ashen-faced, wide-eyed, and gasping for breath.

"What's wrong?" Tuck asked again, hurrying to the monk's side for it appeared he might collapse or faint.

"In there," de Poher said, pointing into the room which Tuck recognised now as the monk's own cell. Although he seemed shocked out of his wits, de Poher's voice had an unusual quality to it, a flat tone that seemed out of place for one so visibly upset. "My God, he's in there!"

TWENTY-SIX

Tuck remained with de Poher, placing a strong, comforting arm around the cantor's shoulder although wincing as he did so for his injured bicep was beginning to ache and he knew there would soon be a great bruise to remind him of the fight.

Little John ducked his head and went through the low door arch into de Poher's chamber with Will directly behind him ready for another altercation but prepared to use deadly force this time.

The cell was furnished with a simple bed, a chest, a stool, and a desk. There was a narrow, glazed window that let in the last of the day's sunshine, casting an orange hue over everything.

"By Christ," John breathed as he saw Brother Magnus and realised why Simon de Poher had come reeling out of the room with such a shocked expression.

"What is this?" Will breathed, swallowing and gaping at the terrible scene before them. "I've never seen anything like it."

"I hope we never see anything like it again!" John murmured, steadying himself against the wall.

Friar Tuck could hear his friends and was alarmed by the emotion in their voices. What could be so horrific, so upsetting, that even those two hardened warriors – who had seen so much death and violence in their lives – would be completely unmanned by the sight of it?

"Sit down, brother," Tuck said to de Poher and helped him slump to the ground where he would not faint and hurt himself although, again, the friar was struck by the strange look on his old acquaintance's face. He did not appear as shocked as Will and John sounded, but then again, people did react differently to things and de Poher might well have an extreme, delayed reaction to what he'd witnessed later.

Content that the man was safe enough, Tuck went into the cell to check on his friends who were oddly silent. It immediately became apparent why.

"Holy Mary, mother of God!" the friar burst out, blessing himself and grasping the door frame. "This is an abomination!"

"Truly," Simon de Poher agreed from the corridor.

Tuck steadied himself, breathing slowly and deeply, trying to understand what he was seeing.

On the floor lay Edward Magnus, and he was very clearly dead. The cellarer was in the centre of a bizarre chalk symbol, with candles at the six points, and, most shockingly of all, he appeared to have stabbed himself in the heart with one of the knives all the monks carried. The blade was still lodged within him and his dead eyes stared up at Tuck from the ensanguined floor.

"There's that smell again," Will said, pulling himself together with a visible effort and bending to sniff at the corpse, a sour expression twisting his features.

"And the powder we've seen before," Tuck nodded, pointing at small piles of what looked like blue-grey salt that was scattered around the body. "It must be an important element of this hideous ritual."

He was suddenly reminded of the phrase he'd read days ago in the cellarer's occult tome, the *Necronomicon*: 'Salz des Lebens'. Tuck had forgotten all about that, and he turned and called out through the door to Simon de Poher, asking his friend if he knew what it meant.

"That's German," the cantor shouted back after a short pause. "Salt of Life."

Tuck took that in, gazing down at the piles of dust, suddenly understanding what they were. Powdered bones. God in Heaven, what had the man been attempting to do here? Another thought came to the friar then, as he recalled the writings of the French monk, Ademar of Chabannes. The scribe had recorded a heretic who carried with him a powder made from the ashes of children. Any who ingested this powder would reject Jesus Christ and practice abominations and unspeakable crimes. Had Edward Magnus discovered a similar, blasphemous powder?

"Why would he kill himself though?" Little John asked looking away from the corpse and out of the window, as though the clean, fresh snow might rinse away the sight in the monk's cell. "It makes no sense. He went to so much trouble stealing those pigs and taking them to the hilltop for the sacrifice, and then digging up those bones in the burial ground and all the rest of it. Why do all that, only to stab himself in the heart?"

"He knew we'd discovered his secret underground chamber," Will shrugged, standing and edging backwards to the door as if he expected the cellarer to stand up and come for him. "He knew his time was running out and he'd swing for his crimes, so he did himself in, even though suicide's a cardinal sin."

"A sin?" John's low laugh rumbled from deep in his chest. "I don't think Brother Magnus was too worried about sinning. I mean, look at that. What the hell is that symbol chalked around his body, by Christ!"

"No idea," Will conceded, staring at the design which seemed to be made up of two separate stars but with hooks curving off them at random points. It was certainly not something any Christian would draw.

"He worshipped a different master than the rest of us," Tuck said. "Whether that was Belial, or Satan, or one of the other demons he spoke of to us."

"But why sacrifice himself to…whatever," John asked with a frown, "in Brother de Poher's cell?"

"I believe I can answer that," de Poher himself replied from out in the corridor. "Brother Magnus told me that the priory was built on top of an ancient manor house, or, more accurately, on top of a number of old dwellings. I believe this site was inhabited right back before Roman times, perhaps even by the ancient Britons of Merlin's time."

"So?" Will prompted when de Poher paused for a moment, damp eyes sparkling as he peered into his cell at the dead man.

"Well, I don't know if Brother Magnus had a floor plan of one of the previous buildings that had been here. I think he must have, because he told me that this cell was located directly over the site of some ancient place of power."

"What kind of power?" Tuck asked, eyes narrowed for it seemed Simon de Poher spoke with rather too much confidence about these dark matters. It was quite unbecoming for a monk, and Tuck wondered if his old friend had somehow been infected by the deceased cellarer's interest in the occult.

"Oh, evil power," de Poher replied, shuddering and somewhat setting Tuck's mind at ease. "Men and beasts had been sacrificed to the ancient, pre-Christian gods and goddesses worshipped back then – Hecate and Cybele in particular. Brother Magnus thought there must be great residual power still contained in this area, right here in my cell."

"Did he tell you he planned something like this?" John asked, more sharply than Tuck thought warranted.

"Of course not," de Poher returned coolly. "I returned here after Vespers and found him like that."

"His henchmen let you past?"

"Henchmen, Tuck?" the monk replied, confused. "There was no one here when I arrived. I went inside, saw him lying there, and I must have fainted."

John and Will glanced at one another and Tuck understood their suspicious expressions. Something about de Poher's story did not seem quite right, but the friar knew there was no way his old friend could possibly have stabbed Edward Magnus through the heart. The monk simply did not have it in him to be violent. And besides, only Brother Magnus would have arranged the cell in such a ritualistic fashion.

Simon de Poher was no devil worshipper – this whole thing was on the cellarer, and anything odd about de Poher's story must be down to shock or a simple misremembering of events. Walking into one's own cell to find a dead body would do that to a person, especially a man of peace who'd probably never been exposed to the aftermath of such terrible violence before.

"Are you fit to walk, brother?" John asked, stretching up to his full height and taking command of the situation as befitted his position as a man of the law.

"I think so," de Poher said.

"Then go to Prior Engayne and tell him what's happened here. At least with the death of Brother Magnus the strange events and crimes should be over."

"And we can go home," Will added. "Just in time for Christmas."

"Something to celebrate," de Poher noted, "after all this. Well, I'll go and speak with the prior. You might want to be careful, you three, for I think those men out in the corridor are coming to and I assume it was you who attacked them."

"Other way around," Will objected. "Well, sort of."

Simon de Poher bowed his head and walked away to find the prior, stepping carefully over the prone servants who Tuck and Will moved now to disarm before they came fully back to consciousness.

"I'd tie the bastards up," Will said, glaring down at the skinny man who'd probably suffered the worst injuries. "But after the last time we did that, I'm not sure it's a good idea."

"They're no threat," John said. "Farmers and labourers with no idea how to really fight. And now the man paying them is dead. Send them on their way when they wake up; we've more to think about now than them."

"You think this is all over then?" Will asked, looking from John to Tuck.

"I think Haltemprice Priory will always have a stigma attached to it," the friar replied. "Thanks to the actions of Edward Magnus. But God has prevailed, as I promised he would, and now, aye, Will, I think things will start to get better for the monks and the people in the surrounding steadings."

"Well, there's one more thing we might want to do tomorrow," John said. "Before we leave."

"What's that?" Will wondered, still glaring at the slowly rousing servants on the floor.

"Head down to the undercroft and find Brother Magnus's occult books," the bailiff replied grimly. "And burn the lot of them!"

TWENTY-SEVEN

With it dark outside and nearing bed time for the monks Prior Engayne decided to stick to Haltemprice's usual routine, asking the three friends to keep what had happened to the cellarer a secret for now. When the brothers were attending Compline, the now familiar plainsong filling every part of the priory, Will and John wrapped Edward Magnus's body in a blanket and carried it down to the undercroft. The three servants who'd been murdered down there were now in closed caskets, hidden from sight until the coroner could come and conduct his investigations. There was no spare casket in the room so John told Will to just lay the cellarer's corpse on the ground, and there he was left. They did not even remove the knife from his chest, for the bailiff knew the coroner would want to see it, and record it in his official report.

"God's blood, it already stinks of death and decay in here," Will cursed, covering his nose and mouth with his cloak. "That coroner better turn up soon."

"Not our problem," John shrugged, heading back up to the cloisters and from there out to the guest house. The snow still lay thick on the ground and the wind made both men throw up their hoods, hurrying across the courtyard with thoughts of a good meal and a good night's sleep filling their minds. It had been a long, eventful day, and they'd earned some rest, even if they were disappointed not to get the chance to question Edward Magnus. His motives for what he'd done still baffled John, despite Tuck's insistence that the cellarer had simply sought to gain power by worshipping devils.

The friar was already in the guest house when the others came in. He'd lit the fire so it was nice and cosy in the main room, and was laying out bread, cheese, and fish for supper, along with cups of ale that the prior had sent over to them from the brewer's.

"The lunatic probably believed he would survive stabbing himself in the heart," said Tuck as the famished companions set to their meal with enthusiasm. "He must have thought his master, Satan or whoever, would spare him, but, at the same time, recognise his devotion in performing such an act."

"It's all madness," Will said through a mouthful of buttered bread. "I just don't understand any of it. There are so many questions unanswered."

"I doubt we'll ever get those answers, so we might as well forget about it. Our part here is done, and the priory is safe from that monster." John grinned and popped a chunk of cheese into his mouth, wincing slightly at the strong taste before cutting another, even bigger piece for himself.

"I still think Brother de Poher might have had more to do with everything," Will told them, not quite ready to forget it all as John suggested.

"Simon?" Tuck demanded. "You met the man! Surely you must have seen how anxious, how nervous, he is. He could never have stood up to Edward Magnus, never mind had a part in his death if that's what you're suggesting."

Will shook his head. "I'm not saying he murdered Magnus, but, like you say yourself, de Poher is a nervous person – far more than most. Anxiety can make men do strange things, Tuck, you know that. Make them behave out of character."

"What do you think, John?"

The bailiff turned away from the crackling fire to look at Tuck, taking a long moment to think over the friar's question. "I can see Will's point," he admitted. "And you did tell us that de Poher once shoved someone down a flight of stairs."

"He was *accused* of that," Tuck corrected.

John shrugged. "Like Will says, anxiety – a constant, heightened sense of fear – can make a man behave strangely. Violently, even." He turned back to gaze into the fire. "I think it's obvious Brother Magnus was behind everything, but who knows? Maybe de Poher had a part to play in some of it."

Tuck shook his head in disbelief. "I can't accept it," he said. "You two think Simon is mad at best, or dangerous at worst. All I see is the same anxious monk I knew years back, who simply wants to serve God as best he can."

The three men fell into thoughtful silence for a while and the atmosphere was a little strained until John said, with his usual infectious grin, "Well, I think we can all agree that Edward Magnus was a right arse, and Haltemprice is far better off without him."

"Agreed!" Tuck laughed and the friends raised their ale cups in salute.

"When do we leave for home?" Will asked Tuck.

"Tomorrow, I suppose, if you two are fit enough."

"If we're fit enough?" John demanded incredulously. "You're the one that was in the infirmary this morning. We thought you were dying!"

"The good Lord protected me, as he always has," Tuck said, looking up the rafters with a beatific smile. "I'll be ready to ride back to Wakefield on the morrow, don't worry about me. Well, assuming the roads are clearer than today."

"I think it might rain during the night," Will predicted. "So that will either clear the snow away, or it will turn everything to ice."

"Another day in this guest house won't do us any harm," John smiled. "Not if Prior Engayne is going to keep supplying us with ale and this cheese."

"Nah, I've had enough of this place," Will said, downing a huge mouthful of ale. "The sooner we can leave the madness behind, the better."

"We've still to destroy those old books of dark magic from the undercroft," John said. "I don't know what's in them, but we don't want someone else reading them and going as mad as Brother Magnus did."

"I agree," Tuck nodded. "I looked through them briefly and that kind of knowledge shouldn't just be hidden, it should be destroyed!"

"Then we'll have a nice bonfire before we head for home," said John.

"That's the rain started," Will told them, getting up to peer out the window. "I think we'll be fine to travel in the morning."

"Good," John said, pouring himself another large cup of ale. "But, for now, I intend to get quite drunk. I think we deserve it, lads."

"You've twisted my arm," Tuck replied. "Pour me another too."

"Aye, and me," Will agreed. "It's almost Christmas and I'm ready to start celebrations right now!"

* * *

When they awoke the rain was not as heavy as it had been during the night. Indeed, it had been so hard that it had wakened Tuck at one point, drumming on the roof and windows of the guest house. He was surprised to endure yet another nightmare for he'd believed the end of Edward Magnus would have broken that cycle but apparently not. As ever, he could only remember vague fragments of the dream, but Brother Magnus had been in it, his goatish face smiling malevolently at Tuck as he…Tuck simply could not recall what it was the dead cellarer had been doing in the nightmare, but the friar felt sullied, the fading memory touching some part of his subconscious mind and making him glad it had been repressed.

"Someone was up early this morning," Will Scarlet noted grumpily when the three men arose and sat eating a meagre breakfast, staring out the little windows at the drizzle. They were all nursing hangovers, and the colour did not come back to their faces until they'd forced down a little bread and butter, and half cups of the ale.

"Wasn't me," John said. "I slept like a babe all night."

"A babe that snores like a bloody horse," Will grumbled.

"Wasn't me either," Tuck told his irritable friend.

"I know it wasn't any of us," Will told them, swallowing another mouthful of ale and wincing. "It was one of the monks, heading off on a wagon at the crack of dawn."

"A wagon?" John muttered. "Good luck taking a wagon along those roads."

"Aye, exactly," said Will. "It looked heavily laden too."

Outside, another, different wagon rolled past, drawn by a pair of oxen and carrying food for the refectory's stores. Clearly the roads were not completely impassable.

"Let's get moving," John suggested. "We need to finish off here by burning those evil old books, and then begin the journey home. We're going to need to camp at least one night, but I'd rather be able to choose a decent spot than be forced to stop wherever we are when the light fails."

The three friends had all their belongings packed and ready to travel having done it the night before while making merry, so they simply threw on their cloaks, made sure their weapons were in place, and left the cosy guest house to head for the main priory buildings.

"It feels noticeably cheerier around here," Tuck noted as they reached the entrance and were met by a pair of smiling novices who were decorating the doorway with holly and ivy. Inside, the sound of more monks chattering and some even singing carols could be heard as they went about their duties.

"Quite a difference," Will nodded, eyeing the novices as if he half expected them to attack them at any moment. It truly was an incredible transformation.

"Seems the death of Brother Magnus has lifted the pall that lay across Haltemprice," Tuck grinned and went inside, shaking the light smirr of rain from his cloak.

"Let's just head straight down to the undercroft," John suggested. "And deal with the books. If we ask for permission we might not be granted it. We still have the keys from the sacrist."

"He'll be after our blood if we don't return them to him soon," Tuck smiled. "But I agree. Let's do it."

No one challenged them as they went past and unlocked the door to the undercroft. They were even handed candles by one of the monks who saw where they were going and within moments they had descended the stairs and made their way to the dead cellarer's work room.

"The books," Tuck said, running to the shelves that had once contained a dozen or so large tomes but were now completely empty. "They're gone! Look, even the metallic apparatus Magnus used for his experiments has disappeared."

"Ah, shit," John groaned. "Someone must have realised the things were valuable and took them all away for safe keeping. This is going to make life harder."

Will Scarlet shrugged, seeming bored by the whole affair now. "Who cares?" he asked, turning and leading the way back to the cloisters. "We tried. If someone wants to keep those evil old books around, that's up to them. I'm just looking forward to getting home to Wakefield, seeing my wife and son, and enjoying a pleasant yuletide!"

They trudged back up to the cloisters and were told by a novice that Prior Engayne was in the chapter house, working. Sure enough, they found the elderly clergyman there, looking happier and more relaxed than he had in the short time they'd known him.

"We were planning on destroying the old occult books belonging to Brother Magnus," Tuck told the prior without much preamble. "But they're gone."

"Gone? Where to?"

"No idea," Tuck told him. "We thought you might know. Those books are filled with evil, Father. They should be burned."

"I'm not disagreeing with you, Brother Tuck," the prior admitted. "But I've no idea who could have removed those books."

"Who left on the wagon this morning?" Will asked, frowning suspiciously. "That thing was heavily laden. The books might have been on there, Father."

They were not prepared at all for the reply when it came.

"That was Brother de Poher," the prior told them. "He decided to leave us after yesterday's shocking events."

"What? Just like that?" Little John demanded. "Bit sudden, is it not?"

"Not exactly," Prior Engayne sighed. "Brother de Poher has been offered a more prestigious position at another abbey. He had a letter confirming it from Bishop de Egglescliffe who, apparently, sponsored him weeks ago. After yesterday's trouble, Brother de

Poher decided to accept the offer. He left for Fance this morning."

TWENTY-EIGHT

The prior ordered his monks to turn the place upside down, searching for the *Necronomicon,* and *De Vermis Mysteriis*, and all the rest of the blasphemous tomes that had belonged to Brother Magnus. Although Prior Engayne was not entirely convinced that they should be burned – they were extremely valuable after all, and destroying any book was anathema to a learned man – he agreed that they should at least be kept hidden from unwary delvers into the occult. It was quite possible the arcane secrets contained within the likes of *The Black Book of Azathoth* had contributed to the cellarer's descent into madness and depravity, and such knowledge, said the prior, should be locked away from those too weak of mind to comprehend it.

Not a trace of any of the books was found and Tuck said what they had all been thinking: "Brother de Poher must have taken them with him, as Will suggested."

"But why?" Prior Engayne asked. "He wasn't the sort to be interested in heretical books. Quite the opposite in fact."

"That's true," the friar admitted. De Poher was a singularly unimaginative man – the thought of him stealing a dead man's expensive books and smuggling them out of the priory to take to France was incredible. Then again, his dawn journey had come completely out of the blue as well… "Did you notice anything different about him since yesterday, Father?"

The prior stroked his freshly-shaved chin and pursed his lips thoughtfully. "Well, he'd had a terrible shock, finding Brother Magnus dead in his cell like that. So, yes, he did seem a little off, but it's to be expected. He must have been out of his mind."

"Maybe," Will Scarlet murmured. "But I've seen plenty of men after a shock, and Brother de Poher's reaction was probably the strangest of them all. It was almost as if he was a different person."

Tuck murmured in agreement. "Taking valuable books that weren't his and riding off at the crack of dawn to sail for a new country is, well, it's utterly bizarre. Completely out of character for Simon."

"I agree, but Haltemprice has seen quite a few bizarre things lately," the prior replied with a bleak smile. "What's one more?"

"Hang on," John interrupted. "There's one place we haven't searched."

"That charnel house beneath the priory?" Will asked after a moment's thought. He did not look pleased at the idea of heading back down to the hellish underground vault.

"Aye," John nodded. "We know the cellarer conducted his strange rituals down there. Wouldn't it make sense for him to have some of those damned books with him? Remember, he ran for his life when he saw us – he didn't have time to collect anything, and we never searched the place because the candles blew out." He turned to the prior, anxiety at returning to the Chamber of Bones mingling with excitement at what they might find if they were to search the place thoroughly. "Did you have anyone go down there yet?"

"No!" Prior Engayne replied. "From what you say it's the last place we should be delving into. The coroner can go down when he finally turns up, if he wants, but I have no intention of subjecting myself, or anyone else, to that place of death."

"You have no objections to us taking a proper look?"

"None," said the prior. "If that's what you want to do, I'll pray for your safe return."

"Oh, Christ, not again," Will groaned, looking up at the ceiling as if imploring God to spare him from a return visit to the huge chamber.

"Don't worry, we'll take proper lamps with us this time," John promised. "Plenty of them."

"I'll have those prepared for you," said Prior Engayne. "When will you go down?"

"Now," John said. "Before we change our minds!"

The prior nodded, clearly impressed by the bailiff's courage. "Fortify yourselves, my friends, with some of our wine. There's some in that chest there. I'll return once your lamps are ready."

The companions did look out the wine, pleased to find it was of the very best quality. They did not drink too much though, knowing they'd need clear heads for the coming task so, by the time they were in the undercroft once more and ducking their heads to enter into the tunnel, they felt braver, but not drunk.

They moved quickly, the light sources provided by Prior Engayne giving them confidence. Not only had he given them a couple of oil lamps, but also a pair of lanterns crafted by one of the monks after an old design credited to Alfred the Great. With thin pieces of bone to let out the candlelight, it also stopped wind from blowing out the flame. So armed, the three friends felt rather more confident as they stepped out of the cramped tunnel into the soaring vault with its carpet of rat-gnawed human bones.

"Let's hurry up," Will said in a low voice, eyes darting from one shadowy side of the room to the other. "Magnus isn't likely to have stashed valuable books out there in the edges of the chamber. If his books are here, they'll be down there in that pit with the altar we saw him conducting his ritual over."

"Leave one of the lanterns here," suggested Tuck. "It'll show us where to walk to on our way back."

Silently, the trio made their way gingerly across the skittering, clattering remnants of once-living men and women, cringing, desperate not to fall. At last they made it to the place where Edward Magnus had stood, talking to his invisible friend, Ecgbert.

"There's that weird salt again," said Will, face screwing up at the pungent smell. The powdery substance lay on the ground in the centre of another chalked symbol, and there was a lot of it, hence the strong scent. "What the hell is it?"

"It's the same colour as bones," John noted, looking at the odd, pungent dust and back at the many pale, scattered skeletons that populated the vault.

"Indeed," Tuck replied. "That's exactly what it is, pulverised bones, perhaps mixed with some other chemical that gives it such a powerful smell. He's been using that salt for something, but I'm not sure what."

"He was a necromancer," Will said with sudden insight. "He's been trying to bring people back to life using their bones. That's why he wanted those from the old Saxon burial ground."

"Maybe that's who the voice belonged to when we heard the conversation here," John murmured, shuddering at the implications. "Ecgbert was some predecessor of his. A black sorcerer. That must be why his bones were buried in the shunned cemetery!"

Tuck found it all too incredible to believe, and yet, there had been two very distinct voices in that conversation they'd overheard down here in the vault. Was it possible for a necromancer to revive a person long dead? Perhaps not their body which had decayed beyond repair, but their essence? Even just for a short time, long enough for one to converse with them, and learn knowledge that had been lost for aeons?

"Let's get out of here," the friar said to his friends. "There's nothing more to find, and we have much to think on."

TWENTY-NINE

The atmosphere around the priory was joyous as Tuck, John and Will collected their belongings and left the guest house for the ride back to Wakefield. The sun was shining, birds were singing in the herb garden, and the garlands of greenery that had been hung around the outsides of doors and windows gave the place a festive feel.

"I think it's safe to say the blight that affected this place has gone," Tuck said to Prior Engayne as the companions waited for their horses to be brought out to them by the stablehands.

"The evil has gone," the prior agreed, blessing himself with a relieved smile. "Thank you, brother, and your friends, for your help. If you hadn't come I dread to think what the end result of Edward Magnus's unearthly experiments might have been."

"What will you do now?" Will asked. "I'd suggest you destroy the storehouse with the entrance to the Chamber of Bones and let the grass grow over it so no one ever finds it again."

Prior Engayne nodded. "Once the coroner has been that is exactly what we'll do." He let out a long, heavy sigh and raised an eyebrow at Tuck. "I suppose it's my duty to go down there and conduct a blessing for the souls those bones belonged to. Hopefully let them rest in peace. After that, I'll have it sealed forever. With God's blessing our priory will thrive after that. It's certainly been a troubled start for us so far, but I'm hopeful things will improve now."

"You'll be in my prayers too, Father," Tuck promised. "And I'm glad we were able to help."

The stablehands brought their horses and the sullen looks the men had worn just a few days before were gone, replaced by respectful bows and deferential smiles. It truly was remarkable the change that had come over Haltemprice Priory with the death of its cellarer, and it proved to everyone that God would always triumph over evil in the end.

With happy farewells ringing in their ears, and packs full of victuals provided by the monks, the companions rode through the gates and took the road to the south. The earlier rain followed by the current bright sunshine had made the roads damp but they were able to make good time and it wasn't long before they came to the fork that would carry them westwards, to home.

"What's that up ahead?" John asked. Since he sat higher in the saddle he was able to see things before the others, and he was able to recognise the familiar shape of a wagon, apparently stuck by the side of the main track.

"Trouble?" Will asked as they rode up beside the wagoner who was cursing and sweating as he tried to repair a damaged wheel.

"Aye," the man replied, glancing back at them, red face covered in a sheen of sweat. "Got stuck in the mud and then this happened. You couldn't help me out, could you? I need the wagon lifted so I can knock the peg back into place."

"Aye, friend, no problem," said Will, dismounting and placing his hands beneath the wagon which was not loaded. When John and Tuck were beside him, the three were able to easily lift the vehicle, allowing the wagoner to thump the peg that secured his wheel back into place.

"Thank God you turned up," the man said, smiling gratefully at them. "I've been stuck here for bloody ages. Just didn't have the strength to lift the thing on my own."

"At least there wasn't a full load stowed on board," Tuck said. "Made it lighter for us."

"It was loaded when the wheel first came off," the wagoner grunted, pushing himself back to his feet and eyeing his repair with grim satisfaction. "I asked my passenger to help me fix it, but he refused. Lazy bastard. And then another cart came along carrying wool to the port at Kingstown-upon-Hull, my passenger transferred his stuff to that one, and off they went. Not very Christian behaviour if you ask me. You'd expect better from a monk."

"A monk?" Tuck asked, and Will cried out, a finger raised in the air in recognition.

"You're the wagoner that was at Haltemprice Priory this morning," Scarlet said. "I knew you looked familiar. You took Simon de Poher."

"Aye, that was me. I was paid to take him and his belongings to the port, but this happened"— he kicked the wheel in disgust — "and now I've lost a whole morning and not been paid a penny for my time."

"What belongings did he have?" Little John demanded.

"You know," said the wagoner with a shrug. "Some clothes, food and drink, quite a bit of coin actually, more than I'd have expected a monk to own.

Oh, and a great bloody chest full of books and some copper tubes and stuff. Weighed a ton, I couldn't lift it myself, a couple of monks at the priory had to help me get it on board."

"Did you see the books?"

"No, brother," the man said to Tuck. "The monk warned me to take good care of them though. 'You look after this chest, you dullard,' he says to me, 'or things will go badly for you. These things have been in my possession for decades.' Bloody pompous arsehole. I hope his ship sinks and all his books are lost in the Humber."

Tuck, John, and Will all looked at one another and the friar felt bile rise in his throat. Simon de Poher had not owned those books for decades, but Edward Magnus had.

"I think we need to delay our return home," said John, as if reading Tuck's mind.

"Well what are you waiting for?" Will shouted, already mounted on his horse. "We need to get to the port before those books are out of our reach forever!"

THIRTY

Tuck's mind was reeling as they pushed their horses towards the docks, hooves thundering on the soft roads and tracks. Why was Brother de Poher leaving like this, in such a hurry? And why had he taken – stolen, really – Edward Magnus's books of forbidden lore? Had the shock of finding the cellarer dead snapped de Poher's mind? Tuck had known men to act strangely after witnessing terrible violence, but this seemed different. This behaviour was totally out of character for the quiet, introverted de Poher. This was more like the kind of thing a confident, worldly man would do, not someone who'd spent his whole adult life living in priories or abbeys, being guided in almost every action by his superiors.

It did not matter – Tuck and his friends simply wanted to find those unholy books and dispose of them. With Edward Magnus's death they legally belonged to Haltemprice Priory, and Prior Engayne had given them permission to dispose of the volumes as they saw fit.

The quiet, rural roads eventually gave way to more densely populated ones leading towards Kingstown-upon-Hull, with merchants, traders, pedlars, and workers travelling to the town on foot, by horse, or in wagons.

"Clear the way!" John roared, his great booming baritone drawing the attention of everyone blocking the road. "Clear the way for the law!"

There were angry glares from the people letting the three riders through, and even some shouted insults, but none sought to bar their way and soon the bailiff was leading them through the town gates and towards the docks.

"We could spend hours searching here for him," Will said, running his eyes from one end of the port to the other. It was busy even at that early hour as ships loaded and unloaded their wares: wool, fish, grain, furniture, pottery, passengers, and more. "And we can't just gallop up and down, we'll be arrested."

"Leave the horses," John told them, dismounting and tying his own animal to a post. "We'll get them later. You start at the far end, Will. I'll go to the other end, and you look here for de Poher, all right, Tuck?"

Tuck nodded and moved into the crowd of people, eyes searching for his old friend. They'd been told de Poher's destination was France, so he must be going by a large ship, not some smaller fishing boat or the like. That narrowed things down at least.

"Hail, fellow! Where are you sailing for today?"

A burly sailor who was just about to lift a cask of ale or wine and load it onto his ship looked up at the friar's question. "Norwich, brother," he replied respectfully.

"Damn it. D'you know of any ships heading to France?"

"No, sorry," the sailor told him, lifting the heavy cask of drink and carrying it away.

Moving on, Tuck muttered to himself, cursing Edward Magnus for what he'd done, and Simon de Poher for this goose chase. The friar had been greatly looking forward to supping an ale in Wakefield's tavern on the morrow, not wasting a day's travelling by hunting around these docks for a man he'd barely seen in decades and felt he knew not at all any more.

Then his eye alighted upon the tonsured head of his quarry and relief flooded through him. That pleasant sensation was short-lived however, as Brother de Poher was angrily ordering a couple of sailors around and Tuck noticed the monk was standing aboard a ship with his swarthy companions and the vessel was already pushing off from the docks. The reason for de Poher's fury quickly became apparent, as a crane that was loading a large chest onto the slowly departing ship had not quite placed its load into the keel.

"My books are in there!" de Poher was shrieking, eyes bulging, flecks of spittle flying from his mouth. Tuck had no idea the man had such passion bottled within him, and it spilled over into even louder cursing and blasphemous oaths as the chest hit the side of the ship, tilted, and then fell onto the deck, but not before one of the precious tomes dropped out.

Tuck held his breath, fully expecting the book to land in the Humber with a terrific splash, but it did not. Somehow it sailed through the air and bounced onto the docks just as the friar reached it.

"Well, should we go back for it?" one of the sailors was demanding, also enraged, unused to being shouted at by a skinny monk.

"No," retorted de Poher, meeting Tuck's eyes, a crooked smile curling his lip. "Leave it."

John and Will arrived then and John cursed as he saw the ship carrying the monk out of their reach. The chance to question de Poher was gone now, probably forever, along with any chance of figuring out what had been happening at Haltemprice Priory.

"What's that?" Will asked as Tuck bent and lifted the book that had fallen from de Poher's great chest.

"One of Edward Magnus's magical grimoires I believe," said the friar, holding the book gingerly, fearing it might somehow infect him or burst into hellfire at any moment.

"Toss it in the river then," Will said, slowly backing away from his friend.

"Don't be daft," John laughed. "We came all this way to get hold of those books and God himself laid this one in our lap. I say we take a look."

Brother de Poher's ship was rapidly disappearing to the east and Tuck could not see his old acquaintance any more. He did not expect to ever see him again and he realised that John was right. It was incredible that this one book had fallen out of the chest, and even more miraculous that it had not fallen in the Humber's brackish waters. God had rescued this particular volume for a reason.

"All right," the friar agreed. "But not here. Let's get on the road back home to Wakefield. We can look at the book when we make camp."

"In the dark?" Will demanded, clearly thinking Tuck had taken leave of his senses.

"We'll have a fire," John laughed, slapping Will on the back and leading the way towards their horses. "And I'll protect you from any demons, don't be frightened."

"I bloody well am frightened," Will retorted, shaking his head as he followed his friends away from the docks and eyed Tuck who shoved the grimoire into the pack on his horse. "And I don't mind admitting it."

"Well, you and Tuck are, or were, clergymen," John said, grunting as he hauled himself onto his horse. "Pray for God's protection when we sit down and look in that book."

THIRTY-ONE

The road to Wakefield was a familiar one to all three men and they felt the pull of home ever more strongly the closer they got. Unfortunately, at that time of year the sun went down early and it became dangerous for the horses to travel in the near-total darkness. It was cloudy and had started to snow lightly by the time the companions made camp for the night. They went about their tasks efficiently – setting up tents, gathering firewood, lighting the fire, and making sure the horses were settled – but with their eyes constantly straying towards the pack which held Edward Magnus's book.

"It might not even be anything to do with the occult," John said as he arranged the tripod over the fire and dug out some of the meat the kitchener at Haltemprice had packed for them. He skewered the pieces and set them cooking, the delicious smell filling the frosty air and making Tuck's mouth water.

"Whatever it is," said the friar, taking out a slab of butter and slathering it onto three large chunks of bread. "We'll find out soon enough."

"Should we look now?" Will Scarlet asked, still visibly fearful but also curious. "Or wait until we've eaten?"

In the end they decided to wait for they were hungry and Tuck refused to thumb through what might be a valuable book with butter and grease-stained hands, even if they did plan on burning the repulsive thing eventually. At last, bellies filled and aleskins within easy reach, the portly friar rinsed his hands in the beck that burbled beside their campsite, dried them off on his grey robe, and drew out the book that had fallen from Simon de Poher's chest.

Glancing at his friends, Tuck felt their trepidation. He, and they, had fought many earthly battles over the years, taking near-fatal injuries in the process, yet this book frightened them more than any mortal enemy.

"Glory to the Father, and to the Son, and to the Holy Spirit," the friar intoned, grasping his cross and closing his eyes. "As it was in the beginning, is now, and ever shall be, world without end. Amen."

His friends murmured the words along with him and then, drawing in a deep breath, Tuck grasped the book and opened it close to the fire, its glow casting a ruddy, almost hellish light upon the first page.

"Oh," said Tuck, surprised. "It doesn't seem to be a grimoire after all. It's a journal."

"A journal?" Will asked in a hopeful tone. Surely that couldn't be as dangerous as some book of evil magic.

Tuck grunted agreement and began to read. It was written in Latin, and the ink appeared fresh.

"What does it say?" John asked, leaning over the try and catch a glimpse of the pages himself although he would not be able to understand any of it.

"It seems to be a record of experiments conducted," Tuck said, a deep frown furrowing his brow. "Of rituals conducted by, I assume, Edward Magnus." He read on, nodding and muttering to himself. "Yes, he describes Haltemprice Priory just as we saw it, with the underground vault, and the second entrance to it." He trailed off and remained silent for a long time as he scanned the pages, feeling ever more disgusted by what was recorded in that vile journal.

"Come on, Tuck, what does it say?" Will demanded. His fear had given way to curiosity and he too was staring down at the vellum pages of the journal, the scrawled words seeming to writhe in the flickering firelight as though they had some dreadful life of their own.

"Oh, God and the saints preserve us," the friar groaned as he reached the end of the book and held a hand up to his face, sorrow filling him. "If this journal is accurate, Edward Magnus is not dead after all. My old friend, Simon de Poher, is though."

THIRTY-TWO

"What are you on about?" Will asked, chuckling in disbelief. "We saw Magnus's body. He had a knife through his bloody heart! He's as dead as anyone can possibly be. We carried his corpse down to the undercroft ourselves."

"Aye," John agreed, looking at Tuck as though the friar had lost his mind. "And we literally just saw Simon de Poher sailing away down the Humber just a few hours ago. What are you saying?"

Tuck put down the book and stood up stiffly, stretching out his neck and rolling his shoulders. He'd been reading the journal for longer than he realised and he wished he could jump in a river and wash away the taint of its satanic scribblings.

"We all noted the change in de Poher outside his cell, didn't we?" he asked. "When we found Magnus's body."

"Aye, we put it down to the shock of what had happened," John nodded, looking up at the portly friar.

"It was more than that," Tuck replied, fighting to keep his voice calm. "He acted completely out of character ever since that moment. I knew him years ago, and I spoke with him more recently when I first arrived at the priory, and he was the same quiet, introverted monk he'd always been. *That* Simon de Poher would never have left the safety of Haltemprice and his brothers to go off alone on a ship to France. It's completely unthinkable."

"Yet," Will returned levelly. "He did."

"No, Scarlet," Tuck said. "Simon de Poher is dead. Edward Magnus is in control of his body now."

"What?" Little John and Will both burst out laughing and got to their feet.

"It's true," the friar argued, understanding their amusement but utterly convinced he was right. "The book confirms it."

"Come on now, Tuck, you'll have to explain this to us." John reached out and gripped his friend's shoulder almost sympathetically, the way one would do to a confused child or doddering crone. "Men can't simply move from one body to another. It's lunacy to think so."

"I would have agreed with you, right up until the events of the last few days," Tuck replied with a sigh. "But now…" He shook his head and sat back down by the fire, pulling his cloak tighter around his neck as the light snowfall continued. "The journal explains it all. Sit, and grasp your aleskins, lads, and I'll tell you what it says."

The smiles had faded from the faces of the other two and they took their places beside the campfire again, disturbed by how earnest their old friend was.

"Brother Magnus was a necromancer," Tuck began. "He spoke with the dead. He was speaking with one of them when we found him in the Chamber of Bones, remember Ecgbert? Well, Magnus had discovered a way to commune with those long departed from this world by collecting their bones, reducing them to what the *Necronomicon* called, in German, 'Salz des Lebens' — the Salt of Life."

"This is madness," Will breathed, staring into Tuck's eyes. "You really believe all this?"

"I do now," the friar replied bleakly, before continuing. "Edward Magnus's ultimate goal was to discover a way to transfer his consciousness from his body to another. It required four rituals, and you know about those: the pigs, the murdered servants, the one in the underground vault with the stolen bones, and the final one…."

Grunts of assent.

"Magnus's delvings were the cause of the pall that hung over Haltemprice Priory. He was bringing some demon closer, that he might use its power to switch bodies. I don't know if he always planned on taking poor de Poher, but when we began closing in on him, Edward Magnus knew he had to act. He prepared de Poher's cell for the final ritual and then, when everything was ready, Magnus stabbed himself through the heart and his consciousness switched places with de Poher's."

"This is madness," Will repeated, gazing into the flames. "It has to be."

"Madness or not," John said. "The question is: what can we do about it?"

Tuck bowed his head and eyed the necromancer's journal venomously. "Nothing," he admitted. "You two don't believe what I've just told you. I doubt anyone else will. And even if they did, Edward Magnus will be in France soon enough and completely out of reach."

"The oppressive atmosphere did lift from the priory," John said thoughtfully. "So maybe what you say is true. If so, it's a real kick in the stones to know that murdering bastard Magnus has escaped justice, and moved on to maybe continue his black rituals elsewhere."

"What about Simon de Poher?" Will wondered.

"Dead," Tuck said sorrowfully. "I'm sure of it. God rest his soul. I will ask Father Myrc to say a Mass for him when we return to Wakefield."

They sat sipping their ales in silence for a long time, mulling over everything Tuck had discovered in the journal. Was any of it true? Would Edward Magnus continue his evil work in France, switching bodies at will, essentially immortal? One thing was certain: they could not do anything to stop him. They might be well-known, revered even, around Yorkshire and Nottingham, but they wielded no real power. Not enough to persuade anyone to send men across the English Channel to search for a necromancer anyway.

"Look," said John pragmatically. "It's far more likely that Edward Magnus is really dead, and Simon de Poher found this journal and convinced himself he's been possessed by the mad cellarer. Don't you think?"

"That makes a lot of sense," Will agreed, clearly relieved to have this far more prosaic explanation to cling onto. "People go mad all the time, and de Poher *did* suffer a terrible shock. Maybe it was even him that stabbed Magnus in the heart – we know he pushed a man down a flight of stairs years ago. He has a murderous streak in him!"

Tuck did not argue, he merely nodded, happy to let them believe what they were saying, but he was not sure he went along with it.

"We've all let ourselves get carried away with talk of demons and the supernatural," John said. "But everything that's happened can be explained without all that."

"Really?" Tuck returned. "What about my dream that led us right to the secret door to the Chamber of Bones."

"Well, we'd all been down in the undercroft and felt that through-draught," the bailiff mused, working things through in his head. "Your unconscious mind put things together and made you dream about there being a hidden doorway in the chamber."

Will grinned. "That must be it," he cried. "I've had dreams like that. Like, I'll lose something and forget where I left it, then I'll fall asleep and wake up in the morning knowing exactly where it is." He tapped the side of his head. "Amazing what we can do when we're sleeping."

"What about the feeling of dread that hung about the priory?" Tuck wondered, shivering as he recalled that horrible sensation. "Even you two felt it."

"Mainly the weather," John said. "It was just turning when we went to Haltemprice, with autumn giving way to winter. Darker nights, stronger winds whistling through doors and windows, and heavy snows." He nodded with conviction. "Add all that to the way Edward Magnus and Simon de Poher were behaving and it's no wonder everyone was on edge."

"Especially when those pigs were slaughtered and all the rest of it," Will agreed, almost desperate to believe his friend's prosaic explanation. "Servants creeping about in the dark, threatening people and trying your cell door in the night, Tuck. I think you're right, John. We've just got carried away with ourselves when everything can be explained naturally."

"Whatever the truth is," the friar said at last, not at all convinced by their arguments. "We helped the monks at Haltemprice Priory to remove the evil that was making their lives a misery, and Edward Magnus no longer haunts English lands, praise God. I think that's all anyone could have realistically done. It is enough."

"It'll have to be," Will Scarlet muttered gloomily. "Won't it?"

With a nod and a sigh, Tuck tossed Edward Magnus's journal into their fire and the companions watched it slowly burn to ash.

THIRTY-THREE

The road to Wakefield was uneventful the following day, and the three friends were soon in their homes and looking forward to enjoying Christmas. Ivy, mistletoe, and holly with bright red berries decorated the houses and buildings all around the village and folk sang carols and wassailed in the evenings, their voices and lanterns bringing cheer to the dark streets and driving away the fearful thoughts of Friar Tuck. The memories of what they'd seen at Haltemprice Priory lingered still, but they began to dim as the days passed and the time of Christ's birth drew nearer. How could anyone be frightened of dark magic and demons in a place so filled with friendship and camaraderie as Wakefield?

He had shed a tear when Father Myrc celebrated a memorial mass for poor Simon de Poher, but Tuck was not the type to dwell on the death of a friend and he enjoyed the advent festivities as much as anyone in Wakefield.

Although he was a friar, a man of God, there was much work in the village that needed to be done and Tuck filled his days not just with prayer and study, but by helping the locals mend fences, repair roofs, gather firewood, brew ale, and a myriad other tasks in preparation for winter and the festive season. Of course, in the evenings, he and his friends would enjoy the companionship and cooking at the local tavern.

There would be fresh ale, tasty stews and broths cooked up by the proprietor, Alexander Gilbert, stories, songs, and, of course, gossip, all while the fire crackled merrily away, driving off the effects of the wind and snow that assailed Wakefield every December.

Christmas Eve was always a fine time in the tavern and this year was no different. John had turned up with his wife, Amber, and Will arrived with his own wife, Elspeth, and their little son, Blase. The tavern, hardly the biggest establishment in England, was filled with song, and laughter and light, as the folk sang a carol in memory of the Annunciation, when the Virgin Mary was told by the angel Gabriel that she was pregnant with the Son of God.

Gabriel, that angel bright,
Brighter than the sun is light,
From Heaven to earth he took his flight,
In Nazareth, that great city,
Before a maiden he kneeled on knee,
And said 'Mary, God is with thee,
Hail, Mary, full of grace,
God is with thee and ever was,
He has in thee chosen a place',
Mary was afraid of that sight,
That came to her with so great light,
Then said the angel, that was so bright,
'Be not aghast, least me most,
In thee is conserved the Holy Ghost,
To save the souls that were forlost.'

It was one of Tuck's favourite Christmas songs, and he sang with gusto, smiling, arms across the shoulders of the patrons on either side of him. When they were finished, Will Scarlet called out to the tavern-keeper, Alexander, that a round of drinks was on him and that brought a chorus of thanks and blessings upon him and his beautiful family.

"By the bones of St Cuthbert," Tuck murmured, looking at John wide-eyed. "The Christmas spirit truly has arrived in Wakefield if Will is buying everyone drinks!"

"Shut up, Tuck," Scarlet called, hearing the friar even over the chatter and banter of the packed tavern. "Or I'll tell Alexander to give yours to the old tinker in the corner there." He pointed at a hooded fellow who'd kept himself to himself throughout the festivities, joining in with the carol but only offering a flash of a smile from beneath his hood to the occasional charitable person who stood him an ale.

"Be kind, Will," Elspeth scolded her husband, and Scarlet gaped at her, and then at John and Tuck indignantly.

"'Be kind'! I've just bought everyone in the tavern a drink, and she tells me to 'be kind'."

Elspeth laughed and pulled his head down to give him a quick kiss. "I'm going to Amber's with Blase now, all right? We've a pie to bake in time for tomorrow's feast. I'll see you back at the farm. Don't be getting too drunk!"

"Me?" Will laughed. "Never."

Grinning, Little John kissed his own wife and the ladies took their leave, Will's little boy capering out behind them into the snow, singing the Annunciation carol in sweet, melodious tones that Tuck believed actually brought a tear to Scarlet's eye. No wonder, thought the friar, who knew the sad story of Will's early life and rejoiced that his friend had found love and happiness again.

The tinker wasn't the only traveller in the tavern that Christmas Eve. A pedlar had arrived in Wakefield early that morning and, after visiting every house and business in the village selling or trading his wares, he'd sought solace from the chill in a mug or four of warm ale.

Alexander Gilbert's tavern did not have beds for travellers, being not much bigger than a house and certainly nowhere near as large as the inns one might find in a city. On a frosty night like this, however, a pedlar could spend the night on one of the benches or even on the floor beside the hearth for little more than the price of a few ales. It was far better than sleeping in a tent in the snow.

Of course, that meant visitors could sit for longer, imparting any news or gossip they'd heard on their travels. And pedlars were always a fine source of rumours and tales from abroad.

This one was no different.

"Where have you come from?" Tuck asked as the patrons huddled about the fire, the wind whistling through cracks in the walls and shutters.

"South," the pedlar replied, happily sipping another ale. He was middle-aged with a bald head and grey stubble that somehow gave him a distinguished look. Well, for a pedlar at least.

"Well, we guessed that," Will replied with a laugh. "Whereabouts?"

"Oh, all over," the pedlar said, waving a hand enigmatically. "I'm from London, and I started out there a few weeks back, working my way north until I found myself here in this fine town on Christmas Eve. And a better place to spend such a day a man could not wish for!" He thumped his mug on the bench next to him and the patrons cheered in agreement.

"What news have you heard?" John asked. As a travelling bailiff he often heard of tidings, good and bad, before others in the village but, since he'd been away at Haltemprice recently, he was no wiser than anyone else in Wakefield.

"I've spent the past hour or so telling everyone the news I've heard on my travels," the pedlar replied, scratching his stubble and shrugging apologetically. "I doubt you lads will want to hear anything I haven't already told. Not on Christmas Eve anyway."

"Why not on Christmas Eve?" Tuck wondered.

"Well, it's a holy time, isn't it?" said the pedlar. "Not a time for strange tales of heretics and blasphemy."

Tuck, Will, and John all sat up straighter on their stools, sharing curious looks at the bald man's words.

"What blasphemy?" Will Scarlet demanded, and his tone was so commanding that the pedlar also straightened his back. "Spit it out, man. Christmas or no, we want to hear it."

It seemed the three friends weren't the only ones interested in the tale, for everyone in the tavern leaned in to hear.

"Well," the pedlar said somewhat embarrassed. "There's not much to tell. I just heard in one of the port towns not far from here that there's been some strange business somewhere in France."

"What sort of strange business?" Tuck asked, eyeing the bald man intently.

"Well, some abbey over there has been struck by a run of bad luck recently," said the pedlar, and he lowered his voice conspiratorially, as though he'd only just remembered that the price of his night's lodging, and continued free drinks, might depend on how well he entertained the other patrons. "A couple of monks have died. One even went mad."

Not getting the excited reaction he'd perhaps expected, the pedlar went on, still in the throaty, portentous tone of before. "Word is," he said, "there's been some weird sacrifices. Devil worship. Animals have gone missing from the towns close to the abbey! It's a bad business, I tell you."

"Has anyone been arrested?" Will asked, face pale.

"I don't think so," the pedlar hedged. "Maybe they have been since I first heard about it."

"Bloody French," someone said from amongst the crowd of drinkers. "Always up to weird shit."

There was a chorus of nervous laughter and agreement, but the pedlar shook his head and Tuck felt a shiver run down his spine as the man stroked his grey stubble and said, "Nah. Word is, all the trouble started when some English monk joined the abbey."

Little John appeared at Tuck's side and laid a heavy, reassuring hand on the friar's shoulder. "It's not our problem anymore," said the bailiff firmly. "We did all we could. It's up to the French to deal with him now."

Tuck sighed and nodded, but then he said to the pedlar. "D'you know which abbey this is happening at?"

"Nah," the man replied. "I couldn't pronounce it even if I did. Now, who's for a game of dice?"

The gamblers amongst the patrons broke off to try and win some coins from the pedlar while John and Tuck sat with Will at one of the benches near the hearth. Already some of the drinkers had headed out into the night to make their way home. Why spend their own money on ale when the local lord would be paying for the feast and the drinks tomorrow, on Christmas Day? There wouldn't just be ale, there'd also be wassail – hot, mulled cider, a favourite of Tuck's especially and perfect for this chilly time of year.

"We're not going to France," Will said, glowering at Tuck who, in fact, had been thinking of making just that suggestion.

"No, I suppose not," the friar conceded then, sucking a breath through his teeth he shook his head sadly. "I wish we knew what abbey it was happening at, so we could at least send a letter to them."

"Send it to the pope," John said. "Or the archbishop. They can deal with it."

Tuck thought about the idea but he knew very well that writing such a letter to the most powerful clergymen in all Christendom would probably see him locked up in Bedlam for being a lunatic. The whole story was too incredible to be true, he had no actual proof of his accusations, and, like John said, they had done their bit. The problem of Edward

Magnus/ Simon de Poher was no longer theirs – Tuck, John, and Will's part in the tale was over.

"I don't like it ending in this fashion, though," the friar admitted, supping his ale in hopes it would bring him some Christmas cheer.

"I know what you mean," Will said. "It's nice to tie things up. To have a definite conclusion."

"A happy ending," John nodded. "Especially on this day. For once, we're not getting that, and it does rankle a little."

They sat in silence, staring into their drinks or at the dancing flames in the hearth.

"You three look like you need cheering up," a voice said from beside their table and the friends glanced up. It was the hooded tinker who'd been sitting in the corner throughout the evening.

"Maybe, friend," Will agreed impatiently. "But we're not looking to buy anything."

"Just as well I'm not selling anything then," the tinker replied, throwing back his hood and grinning down at them. "It's nice to see you again, lads. Merry Christmas."

Tuck gaped at the newcomer, thoughts racing, and then, before he realised what he was doing he was on his feet embracing the man, tears of happiness in his eyes as Will and John did the same, all crying out in amazement and joy.

"Robin!" the friar laughed. "It's Robin Hood. You've come home to Wakefield at last!"

TO BE CONTINUED!

AUTHOR'S NOTE

Fans of cosmic horror stories will no doubt recognise some of the elements of this novella. HP Lovecraft's stories, "The Rats in the Walls", and "The Case of Charles Dexter Ward" are huge favourites of mine and I thought it might be interesting to do something similar but in a medieval setting. A new priory built on top of some ancient place of power/burial, and an enigmatic enemy who dabbles in black magic and necromancy? Tuck, John, and Will could certainly have some fun investigating that!

I began by searching for a real priory that wasn't too far from Wakefield and discovered Haltemprice. Originally, the Augustinian priory of St Mary the Virgin and the Holy Cross was founded in 1321 by Thomas de Wake in Cottingham. There were some legal issues however, so in 1325 de Wake moved the whole community two miles south to the settlement of Newton, and the area was renamed Haltemprice. This was the ideal setting for my story, especially as the real priory was badly run, often in debt, and suffered from fire and storm destruction before its dissolution in 1536. I have used some artistic license here as the Augustinians were friars and I wanted monks for this story, so I made them Benedictines (known as 'black monks') instead.

Then, as I was writing the story I realised I wanted to set a chapter at an ancient burial ground. It just so happened that there was a well-known Anglo-Saxon cemetery once known locally as 'Hell's Gate' – the

Walkington Wold Burials – just up the road from Haltemprice Priory. Perfect!

It's odd how often that happens, where I'll need something for a story and, when I research the history, lo and behold, the exact thing I need pops right out at me. I've heard other authors say the same thing, and it's always great when it happens, it makes life much easier and saves you having to invent something. For a writer who tries to make things as historically accurate as possible that's a Godsend.

I must admit, I expected the story to come out at about 25,000 words, but, as usual, it went well over that - almost double! I take that as another good sign – if I wasn't enjoying writing it, I would make damn sure to reach the end as soon as possible. I was clearly having a fine time and hopefully that means readers will also like it.

On the title – yes, it's rather long, but I thought it was good. My editor suggested changing it to *The Chamber of Bones* but I decided to keep it as it is for it fits the story perfectly to me.

Now…that ending! If you've read my Forest Lord novels you'll know how they ended, with Robin apparently dead at the finale of *Blood of the Wolf*. Some people thought he was actually dead, and one guy even thought it was a ghost that climbed into the cart with Matilda at the end! I left it slightly ambiguous because I really didn't want to kill him off – he was still a young guy and I thought there might come a time when he would be needed again by the people of Britain, rather like King Arthur. Well, I think that time has come and, since I wanted to finish *The Heretic of Haltemprice Priory* with the baddie (probably) escaping, I thought bringing Robin back into the fold would be the ideal happy ending. Hopefully you agree.

I've not started work on a new Forest Lord novel yet, and I don't really know when I will, but by using that ending I guess I need to now! What will the plot be? What will it mean for the winter novellas that have now become a tradition? I honestly have no idea, but I'm looking forward to finding out the answers. **They will NOT be travelling to France to chase Brother Magnus though – that story is over.**

Next up will be my third and final King Alfred novel, *King of Wessex*, and shortly after that I plan on publishing the seventh Warrior Druid of Britain novel so keep an eye out for those. As always, thank you so much for reading and, if you enjoyed this book, please do leave a five-star review, it honestly helps me a great deal and is hugely appreciated.

Finally, if you fancy getting into the Christmas spirit even more, check out the brand new Rock, Paper, Swords! song "Wassail The Night Away", available on all streaming services and YouTube. Music by me, vocals by Matthew Harffy, it rocks!

Merry Xmas everyone, and have a fantastic 2025.

Steven A. McKay,
Old Kilpatrick,
October 24th, 2024

THE CHRISTMAS HUNT

by

STEVEN A. McKAY

Copyright © 2023
All rights reserved. No part of this book may be reproduced,
in whole or in part, without prior written permission from the copyright holder.

FOREWORD

I've published a Christmas/winter story every December for the past few years but last year (2023) I wasn't able to (for an explanation why see my Author's Note at the end of the book). I DID write a novelette, *The Christmas Hunt*, and I actually gave it away for free to everyone on my Email List, but it wasn't widely available to the public. Well, now here it is, and I hope you enjoy it. It's not connected to *The Heretic of Haltemprice Priory* other than with the characters. It does take place before the events of the latter tale, but it really doesn't matter which order the stories are read in.

The Chrismas Hunt is a slightly more whimsical, humorous tale – hopefully a nice companion piece for the darker *Heretic*.

Merry Xmas all!

Steven A. McKay

ONE

Wakefield, December 23rd, c. 1330-ish

The villager, a young man with a shock of sandy hair and large sideburns, slammed his palm onto the table making the ale in the mug in front of him slosh over the sides. His face was red with frustration and he let out a bitter oath as he looked up at the enormous man sitting across from him. "I'm done with this, John," the villager groused. "You seem to win every game!"

John Little, the fabled former outlaw who was employed nowadays as a part-time bailiff, raised his eyebrows in an expression of innocent surprise. "I'm just lucky," he replied defensively. "I can't help that, can I, Edward? Blame it on God." Grinning, he reached out, scooped up the two silver pennies resting beside Edward's mug and dropped them into his coin purse. He picked up the dice and rattled them in his hand. "Want another game?" he asked.

"No, I bloody don't," the young villager retorted, standing up and wandering away to sit at another table, leaving the bailiff shaking his head with merriment.

"He thinks you've been cheating," said Will Scaflock, who was also smiling at the lad's display of poor sportsmanship. "A bad loser."

"Me? Cheat? While this fine servant of God looks on? Never!" John reached out and patted the other man left at their table, a rotund, cheery friar everyone knew as Tuck, despite the fact his real name was Robert Stafford.

"No, fair enough," Will admitted. "You're many things – hairy, ugly, smelly, and as stupid as my little dog, Mite – but you're not a cheat."

John eyed his old friend with a mixture of anger and amusement. They'd spent many years in one another's company, as outlaws in the greenwoods of Barnsdale and Sherwood, and latterly as friends on the right side of the law in Wakefield. Humour, sometimes quite vicious humour, had been one way they kept themselves entertained on the long days and nights. One developed a thick skin when it came to Will's insults.

"Stupid, Scarlet?" John demanded, using Will's infamous nickname which had been earned on account of his ferocious temper. "Your dog isn't stupid." He looked down under the table at the little brown terrier lying contentedly at Will's feet and ruffled the dog's ears.

"He is," Will said. "My other one, Holdfast, is much smarter."

"Where is Holdfast anyway?" Tuck asked, drawing his cloak around himself as the tavern door opened and another patron was blown inside in a flurry of snow. "Why did you only bring Mite with you?"

"Holdfast doesn't like too many people around him," Will said. "Doesn't trust them. Mite likes people, which is why he's not very smart!"

"You're a cynical one," John grinned. "Not all people are bad. I mean, you're a twat, but Tuck's alright." He leaned back, still grinning as he looked about the tavern, wondering who might take Edward's place for a game of dice. No-one met his eye, and, when he called out to a few drinkers, asking if they'd play, he was met with blunt refusal.

"See, your reputation's preceded you," Will cackled. "Everyone knows what you're like. No wonder they won't play you."

"Well, what are we going to do for the rest of the night then?" John demanded, putting his dice away in his purse with a dejected look.

"Drink!" Will replied, lifting his ale mug in the air.

"And eat," Tuck added, gesturing to the man behind the bar. "Bring us some of your stew, Alexander," he called. "Make sure it's nice and hot, eh? It's cold out there tonight."

"It is indeed, Brother Tuck," the portly tavern keeper agreed, wandering over to the hearth and putting another log into the flames. "There, that should keep you nice and cosy while I get your food ready. You got enough ale? Aye? Good. I'll be back shortly then."

"Drinking and eating are all very well," John sighed, stretching his enormous legs out beneath the table and placing his hands behind his head. "They're two of my favourite things, to be honest. But I fancy some entertainment. Why are there no minstrels around here?"

"I could sing you a carol," Tuck offered with a glint in his eye. "It's only two days until Christmas after all. What about the one I wrote myself? 'A Child Is Boren Amonges Man'?" Without waiting for an answer he began to sing,

"Hand by hand we shule us take,
And joye and blisse shule we make;
For the devel of helle man hath forsake—"

"No, you're alright thanks, Tuck," Will Scarlet interrupted loudly. "Maybe save your voice for Christmas Day, eh?"

"Aye, you'll drive all Alexander's customers away," John said, and he and Will laughed together like daft boys.

"You can sing hymns any time you like in my establishment, Tuck," the tavern keeper said, bustling over with three bowls of piping hot stew which he expertly placed on the table without spilling a drop. "There you go, lads. Enjoy." He smiled at them, purple nose almost seeming to glow in the firelight, then went off to fill mugs of ale for other patrons as a blast of wind rattled the shutters.

"Since there's no minstrels likely to be on their way here to entertain us in this weather," Will said, "how about we try this thing my old captain used to do with us when I was in the army?"

John and Tuck shared a look then the giant bailiff said with a sardonic laugh, "I'm not sure we want to play those kinds of games, Scarlet."

"Shut up, you bloody oaf," Will retorted. "Look, this is what you do." He gazed about the room, eyes travelling across the patrons drinking at their tables, past the merrily blazing hearth, and on to the tavern keeper who was chopping up winter vegetables ready for his next batch of famous stew. "Right," Will said to John. "You close your eyes. In fact, here, put your cloak on back to front and cover your face so you can't see anything."

"I told you, we weren't playing those—"

"Shut up, John, and do as you're told," Will interrupted. "Go on. You wanted to be entertained didn't you? Well, this always entertained us in the army."

With a slightly worried glance at Tuck who merely shrugged and smirked back, John reluctantly did as he was told, putting his cloak on back to front and pulling up the hood so it covered his face. While he was doing that, Will stood and walked across to Alexander, inspecting the basket of vegetables before finally lifting a carrot and winking at the tavern keeper who stared at him as if he'd gone mad.

"What are you doing," John asked in a muffled voice as Will sat down at the table again. "Better not be any funny business, Scarlet, or I'll punch your fu-—"

"What have I got in my hand?" Will demanded, brandishing the carrot in front of the blindfolded bailiff's face.

John thought about it for a moment, then he said, "How the hell should I know? I can't see anything!"

"Listen, John, I'm going to send you an image of this object, right? Straight into your brain. And you have to tell me what it is, or at least try to describe it. All right? Now, think." Will stared at the carrot, taking in the pointed, purple vegetable with its green top and ridged, earthy body. "Think," he repeated, eyes straining hard at the carrot.

John had finally understood the point of the game and he sat quite still for a long moment before asking tentatively, "A dagger?"

Will looked at Tuck, smiling and nodding.

"Close," he said.

"Close?" the friar demanded. "It's nothing like a dagger!"

"It bloody is," Will replied. "It's a similar shape."

"Pfft, I'd like to see you stabbing someone with that, Scarlet."

"I'll stab *you* with it in a moment, Tuck, if you don't shut up!"

"A sword," John asked.

"No. Think!" Will commanded, staring hard at the carrot again. "I'm sending it to your mind, John. Can you see it? What colour is it?"

John thought about for a long time, really trying to enter the spirit of the game, before he shrugged and said, "Green?"

Tuck laughed, but Will nodded, glaring irritably at the friar. "Part of it's green, aye."

"Holly!"

The tavern was bedecked outside with holly and ivy for the Christmas season, but Will shook his head. "Try again."

"I don't know, this is stupid."

"Try again," Will repeated. "Try to see the image I'm sending into your head."

John sat quietly, picking at the skin on his fingertips, before guessing, "A log for the fire."

"It's a carrot," Tuck said, frowning as Will swore and John pulled the hood down from his face to see the purple vegetable for himself.

"Why did you ruin the game?" Will demanded, brandishing the carrot as if it was indeed a dagger. "It takes time to build a connection between the two people playing. We used to get them right all the time back in my army days."

"It's unholy, Scarlet," Tuck proclaimed as he finished spooning the last of his stew into his mouth.

"What? How's it unholy?"

"It's not natural is it?" The friar was indignant now that his meal was over and he no longer had to concentrate on feeding himself. "You're trying to harness demonic forces to put the images into John's head. It's not Christian."

"Bollocks," Will said hotly. "How d'you know it's not God himself that's putting the image into John's head?"

"Well, if it was, he didn't do a very good job of it," John muttered, beginning to eat his own stew, still with his cloak on back to front.

"Let's try again," said Will. "Come on, once we get a connection, John, you'll be amazed how well it works. You go and pick an object for him to guess, Tuck."

The friar huffed and shook his head muttering that no good could come of such ungodly games, but he got up and looked around the room as John, with loud protestations, stopped eating and covered his face again. Will's little terrier, Mite, jumped up into his lap and sat sniffing at the bowl in front of his master.

Soon, Tuck was seated once more, and holding a jug filled with water which he handed to Will, refusing to take any other part in the game.

"All right, John, what have I got this time?"

Sighing, John held up his palms and tilted his hooded head to the side. "I dunno. A jug."

Will barked with laughter and looked at Tuck. "See? I told you it worked!"

The friar made the sign of the cross towards the jug and muttered a hasty Pater Noster as John pulled down the hood and smiled in disbelief.

"I was right?" demanded the bailiff, as if he'd been tricked somehow.

"Aye, you were right," Will confirmed.

"I saw it," John said. "Like, in my mind's eye, I could see a jug." He shook his head, astonished to have felt this incredible connection with his old companion. "All that time listening to your old stories and putting up with your horrible stench when we were living close together as outlaws in Barnsdale seem to have counted for something, eh, Scarlet?"

"I know," Will nodded. "We must have a bond, John. Mental."

Tuck snorted derisively. "You're mental all right. Both of you." He downed the remainder of his ale and got to his feet, rubbing his belly as he eyed the empty bowl of stew. "That was as tasty as ever, Alexander," he called to the tavern keeper. "I'm for my bed now though, I'll see you all another day. And I'll say a prayer for your souls," he told John and Will. "God grant you a good night."

He went out into the snow, pulling up the hood on his grey cassock as he did so, and then his baritone voice could be heard singing 'A Child is Boren Amonges Man' as he trudged through the darkness towards his quarters in St Mary's.

"You want to try again with a different object?" Will asked John, stroking Mite's head as the little dog licked and nibbled at a paw.

"Aye, let's see if we can repeat our success," the bailiff agreed. "But first, Alexander! You got any of that stew left?"

"More?" Will asked. "You eat more than the friar!"

"Well, I'm bigger than him."

"You're bigger than anyone I've ever met," Will admitted. "You're still a greedy bastard though."

John ignored the insult, pulling his hood up over his face again. "Right, go and find another object then, Scarlet, and I'll try to guess what it is."

By the time Alexander kicked them and the rest of his patrons out into the whirling, glistening white flakes that were quickly forming a blanket on the ground the pair of former outlaws had tried their experiment a number of times.

Had Tuck still been with them he'd undoubtedly have accused them of being in league with Satan, for John managed to guess the mystery object 8 times out of 10, a success rate far higher than chance would allow for.

It truly did seem as if the friends had some kind of strange mystical bond.

TWO

Although thick grey clouds covered the sky the following morning no more snow fell, but the ground was treacherous for man and beast so there were fewer travellers than usual passing through Wakefield that Christmas Eve.

Little John had not heard from Sir Henry de Faucumberg, the Sheriff of Yorkshire and Nottingham, for a couple of weeks so, with no bailiff duties to attend to, he'd spent much of his time decorating his and a few neighbour's houses for the Christmas period.

Those who were too old or infirm to climb rickety ladders in the frost and snow had been glad John was around to hang boughs of holly and ivy on the outside of their doors and windows. It was easy for him as, being so tall, he didn't need to climb on anything to reach the high places. The green leaves and red berries contrasted beautifully with the white, snowy landscape, cheering everyone as they looked forward to the coming holidays.

On Christmas Eve, John spent the morning tidying the houses near his that had lost their holly and ivy in the previous night's wind. He also went out with a shovel and cleared the paths of his elderly neighbours so they could make a visit to the tavern or to buy supplies for the festivities. Considering Little John was widely known throughout all England as either a bloodthirsty outlaw or a no-nonsense bailiff, his own neighbours thought he was just about the nicest man they'd ever known.

"That's a good job you've done this morning," his wife, Amber, told him as he stamped the snow from his shoes and came into their house, ruddy cheeked from the cold. She took his cloak from him and hung it up near the fire so it would be warm if he went out again, then gave him a bowl of hot meat broth and a chunk of black bread to dip into it. "No doubt you'll be wanting to visit the tavern again later on?"

"I don't mind staying home if you want," John shrugged, getting stuck into his meal with relish. His wife was a fine cook, making the best soups and broths even at this time of year when tasty, wholesome ingredients weren't so easy to find. "I was looking forward to trying Will's mind game again though. Why don't you come along with me tonight, and you can see it for yourself?"

"No thank you," Amber replied. "I'm going out myself, to visit some of my friends. Marion, the miller's wife, has brewed some wassail and she's invited a few of us to go along and try it."

John grinned and stopped eating for a moment. "You'll be tipsier than me when you come home then, eh? I remember Marion's wassail last year – the miller could hardly speak after a few cups! You be careful walking home in the dark. The ground's treacherous and it'll likely snow again later. You want me to come and walk you back?"

"Walk me home?" Amber laughed, running a comb through her hair as she sat by the hearth. "Like young lovers? No, the water mill is in the opposite direction to the tavern, I'm sure I'll be fine."

"Well, don't drink too much wassail, I'm looking forward to dinner tomorrow and you know I can't cook as well as you."

"Speaking of which," Amber said, pausing her combing and growing serious. "I wanted to make a cheese tart for tomorrow, but we don't have any soft cheese. Could you—?"

John finished his broth and stood up, nodding. "Market isn't on today," he said, lifting his cloak and pulling it about his enormous shoulders. "But I'll try the baker – he'll probably have some I can buy. We can't have Christmas Day without your cheese tart – old Ivor along the road loves it."

"And you don't?" Amber demanded as he went out the door, ducking so he didn't crack his head off the frame.

"I love everything you bake!" he called over his shoulder and pulled the door shut behind him, stepping out gingerly onto the path, Amber shouting her requirements for the cheese behind him.

There weren't many people out in the streets that day but those he did pass seemed full of Christmas spirit and offered the bailiff hearty greetings which he returned happily. His life was a far cry from when he'd been part of Robin Hood's outlaw band, hiding from the law in the forests, with the constant threat of death hanging over them. From being a 'wolf's head' who any man could lawfully kill, to being a respected member of the community and even a lawman himself, it had been quite a life.

He came to the baker's shop and went in. It was wonderfully hot inside and the baker, Thomas, was there, kneading dough, face red from the warmth of the oven.

"What can I do for you, John?" asked the baker, not stopping his work, pummelling and rolling the lumpy mixture expertly. The man had arms as big as any longbowman and his wife, Joan, who appeared from a room in the back, wasn't much smaller.

"Some of the honey cakes you love so much?" she asked, reaching up and effortlessly lifting down a trencher laden with savouries.

"Well, go on then, just one though," John agreed, patting his belly. "I don't want to get fat. But it's some soft cheese I'm after. We've run out and Amber wants to make a tart for the Christmas feast tomorrow."

Joan nodded and raised a finger. "I know exactly the stuff she means, give me a moment." She placed one of the honey cakes on the counter before him and scurried out the back to the larder, where the cheese was stored to keep it fresh. It wasn't long before she came back with it and handed it to him, telling him how much the two items cost.

He paid and, wishing both a happy Christmas, wandered out into the cold again. After the warmth of the bakery it was quite a shock to stand in the cold street, especially as it had just started to snow again. Pulling his hood up, he bit into the honey cake, savouring the sweetness as he headed back home. As he walked, a red-breasted robin flitted across the ground and landed at his feet, disappearing again in a blur of wings once John had thrown it a tiny piece of his cake. Then, looking up with a smile, the bailiff saw a slim woman in her early thirties walking quickly along the frozen road with a little boy.

"Elspeth!" he called, recognising Will's wife and son immediately.

She turned at his booming shout and her face twisted in what seemed to be a mixture of relief and anxiety. Pulling the child along, she practically ran across to John.

"What's wrong?" he asked.

"Have you seen Will?" she gasped.

"Today? No. Should I have?"

Elspeth shook her head, her eyes roving all about the village and down at little Blase before turning back to John. "We had…I don't know, outlaws or something, at our farm during the night. Will took the dogs and went out to chase them off. Bloody idiot, I told him not to, but you know what he's like. Never one to back out from a fight."

John nodded grimly. Will wasn't known as *Scarlet* for nothing.

"But he's not come home. One of the dogs did, Holdfast, but Will and the other dog are…" Her voice cracked and she looked back in the direction of their farm, tears filling her eyes and pulling Blase in against her so the child wouldn't see her crying. "It's Christmas, John! People are supposed to be kind to each other!"

John reached out with his free hand and put his great arm about her.

"What's wrong, Uncle John?" Blase asked. "Where's my da' gone?"

His high, small voice brought another sob from Elspeth but John grinned and reached down to brush flakes of snow from the boy's hair. "Your da' just went out to chase some silly oafs and got lost in the snow. Don't you worry, lad, I'll soon find him and bring him home."

"Oh, thank you, John!" Elspeth cried, dashing the tears from her face. "I'm worried that..." She broke off, not wanting to alarm her son any more than he already was.

John smiled and patted her arm reassuringly. "I know, the weather makes it more of a worry. But don't fret, I know these lands like the back of my own hand." He held it out to Blase, who eyed it solemnly. "I'll find Will, and if there's anyone trying to be bad to him, they'll get this right across the back of their head!" He mimed slapping someone and pretended to be the victim, sent flying with a daft expression on his face. The boy gave a small chuckle at his silliness which was so at odds with Little John's fierce appearance.

"I don't know what to do now," Elspeth said. "Should I go home, in case Will comes back?"

John shook his head. "Might not be a good idea if outlaws are about. I'll need to go home to get my horse, come with me and Amber will look after you for a bit."

The snow had grown quite heavy now and, by the time the trio made it to John's house it was starting to lie on the ground again. Of course, Amber was friends with Elspeth and welcomed her and Blase into the house, making sure they were comfortable. John strapped on his sword and lifted his enormous quarterstaff then filled an aleskin and packed it along with a loaf of bread into a sack.

"Shouldn't you get the foresters to help look for Will?" Amber asked. Their own son, also named John, was employed as a forester and knew the area around Wakefield as well as any man.

"No time. Not with the weather so bad. Here." Little John handed her the soft cheese he'd bought at the baker's. "Maybe Elspeth and Blase will give you a hand baking that tart. I'm looking forward to tasting it!" He ruffled the boy's hair and, kissing Amber goodbye, promised to be careful and went out to make his horse ready for a journey into the whirling snow.

"God," he said, squinting into the falling flakes as his mount walked through the town towards St Mary's church where Friar Tuck lived. "Why do you always bring us trouble like this when it's snowing and I should be indoors by the fire, supping ale and eating sweetmeats?"

THREE

It didn't take long before John and Tuck had reached the Scaflock farm. They considered taking Will's other dog, Holdfast, to see if it could track its master's last movements, but Elspeth had locked it up inside the house and it didn't seem worth riding back to John's to get the key from her. Most of the dwellings in Wakefield did not have expensive locks, but Will was a wealthy man from his days with Robin Hood, and liked to keep his home secure.

So, without the help of Holdfast, and kicking himself for not bringing the key to let the hound out, John led Tuck to the east, in the direction Elspeth told him Will had gone searching for the troublemakers.

"This snow isn't helping," Tuck groused, as they searched for signs of their friend. They'd tethered their horses in Will's stable and come out to look for footprints or other marks that would lead them to their quarry. Tuck's hood kept blowing down, revealing his tonsured pate which soon became red raw from the cold.

John had a full, unruly head of hair and a thick beard to keep his head warm but he too was feeling the effects of the weather. His hands and feet were numb and, by the time they'd lost sight of Will's farmhouse, the bailiff was shivering, making him fear he was coming down with a fever. "God's blood," he cursed, the words muffled by the falling snow. "Only Scarlet would be stupid or angry enough to go out in this looking for a fight with a bunch of wolf's heads!"

"Aye," the friar agreed, trying once more to get his hood to stay up. "I'm getting too old for this nonsense. Not used to being out in this kind of weather. Still, at least if we get into a fight with some outlaws it'll warm us up!" Like John, Tuck carried a quarterstaff, and he was just as adept at using the massive polearm as the bailiff. They'd spent many hours sparring with one another, and the rest of their gang, over the years, and it had stood them in good stead, helping them survive even when the odds were stacked heavily against them.

Had Will Scarlet finally taken on one fight too many, though? If he hadn't been killed outright by whoever he went hunting for, if he'd been left lying injured somewhere he wouldn't last long in this cold.

"It's starting to stop," John said, looking up at the sky with relief as the heavy flakes were not falling so fast anymore.

"'Starting to stop,'" Tuck murmured sardonically, but was too chilled to make any other comment on his friend's choice of words.

"Aye," John said. "It'll be dark soon though, and we're getting nowhere." He stopped and gazed around at the landscape. All they could see were snow-blanketed fields, and leafless trees. "He could be anywhere."

"Will!"

John flinched as Tuck's voice suddenly boomed out across the land, carrying well enough now that the snow had lessened.

"Scarlet!" John joined in, and then they paused, looking at one another hopefully, straining for some reply. It never came.

"What are we going to do?" Tuck asked. "We could wander around here all day without finding him. He might be in some nearby village tavern, waiting until the weather's better before he comes home of his own accord."

"Aye, or he could be dead and lying underneath the snow right in front of us and we'd never know," John muttered balefully.

Again, they stared at one another, wishing they had some means of locating their old friend, and feeling utterly helpless and impotent.

"Maybe we should go back to Will's house and break the door down," Tuck suggested, turning his back on the wind and hugging himself almost desperately. "Get Holdfast and pray to God the beast can track for us."

John stood in thoughtful silence, knowing it would take a miracle for a dog to find a scent with all the snow to mask it.

"What?" Tuck demanded, seeing John's face suddenly light up. "What have you thought of?"

"I'm just thinking of our game in the tavern the other night," replied the bailiff, and his voice grew more excited as he went on. "We had some kind of connection between us, me and Will, didn't we, Tuck? Even you can't deny it."

Tuck blessed himself and touched the wooden pectoral cross he wore around his neck. "You think you can find him by picturing his location? That's madness, John, and dangerous too. I'm telling you, it's akin to witchcraft and heresy, and you remember how that ended for Lady Alice de Staynton not so long ago, and not so far away from here."[1]

223

"Do you have a better idea?" John demanded, anxiety for his missing friend making him angry with the jovial friar.

"No," Tuck admitted. "But I don't think it'll work. Still, if you want to chance losing your soul to the devil, on your head be it. Go ahead. I'll pray while you do it, and hopefully God will forgive us."

"If God doesn't want us doing it, it won't lead us to Scarlet," John pointed out, and Tuck nodded before taking his cross in his hands and beginning the Lord's Prayer.

John stretched up to his full height, looking at the sky as he silently begged God to help him find Will. Then he closed his eyes and dropped his head, focusing every fibre of his being upon the task at hand.

Little John was not one for much prayer or silent contemplation, so this kind of thing did not come naturally to him, but he instinctively knew that slowing his breathing while shutting out the world around him would somehow open up his mind to receive the information he needed. That was what he'd done in the tavern the night they'd enjoyed so much success, so that was what he did there, in the middle of that remote, snowy field.

Soon, the sounds of Tuck's murmured prayers and even the icy, cutting wind ceased to register in John's mind, and the discomfort in his frozen extremities was forgotten, replaced by a feeling of complete serenity. It was a sensation he'd rarely, if ever, felt in his life before and then, as if placed there by divine hands, Little John saw three trees in his mind's eye,

---

[1] See *Sworn to God*

bereft of foliage, branches stretching up to the sky like bony, eldritch fingers. As he focused on them, relaxed, not trying to force anything, he was somehow on the other side of those trees and looking at a black void in the landscape, just about big enough for a man to fit in.

He opened his eyes with a gasp, shaking his head to clear it, wondering for just a moment where he was and what the hell was going on. And then the image of those trees returned to him, and he gaped at Tuck with an expression of fierce hope.

"I think I know where he is! Come on, Tuck, we have to hurry!"

FOUR

The snow might have stopped but with nothing around to shelter them from the wind it was hard going forging through the thick snow. Little gusts would whip up every so often, blowing frost into their faces and even Tuck was muttering curses as they put one foot in front of the other, heading in the direction of the sun. It still hadn't quite broken through the clouds, and would not before it set, but John walked towards it, much like the wise men made for the star that heralded Christ's birth over thirteen hundred years before.

"Where are we going?" Tuck demanded breathlessly, trying to make out their destination on the horizon. "My feet are so cold, John. I don't know about Will, but I don't think I can survive much more of this without warming up some."

John reached out and patted his friend on the back. "I know, it's hard for you, being so old, but we're nearly there."

"Old?" the friar cried in outrage. "I'm fitter than you! It's just bloody freezing out here and it's not like I had time to look out heavier clothing."

John grinned at him. "Don't worry. Look." He pointed and a wave of relief washed over him for the three trees he'd seen in his mind's eye were visible now. Behind them John knew there was a drop, and a very short distance away a stream snaked through the land.

"Wait, I recognise this place," Tuck said as they trudged closer, cold feet forgotten. "Didn't we—"

"Aye," John said, breath steaming from his mouth as he pushed ever harder through the snow. "We used this place as a camp once when we were outlaws. It's a good place for it, with shelter beneath those trees, and water nearby."

"We should be careful," Tuck cautioned, eyes scanning the landscape warily. "Will was chasing outlaws, you said. Well, it would make sense that he'd end up here, if the wolf's heads are doing as we did, and using this as a place to make camp."

"Good point," John agreed. "I don't want to waste time scouting about though. Will's in grave danger. We'll go quietly, but there's no time to check if anyone's around."

They continued in silence then, the earlier grumbles about the cold and discomfort forgotten as they instinctively moved back into their personas as expert woodsmen. They reached the three trees and halted, crouching down and hiding behind the trunks. It was getting dark already, the sun hidden by a larger forested area a mile or so in front of them.

John looked at Tuck and the friar slowly shook his head, lips pursed. John nodded, he could hear no signs of human activity either. Raising a hand for Tuck to remain where he was, the bailiff slowly, silently moved forward until he could see over the ridge the trees stood on. Below was the site he remembered from years ago, and signs that it had indeed been used recently as a camp. There was evidence of a fire that had burned within the past day or two for it had not been covered entirely by snow. There were also a couple of crude shelters and even a small barrel which most likely had contained ale but would surely be empty now.

"It looks abandoned," John said, standing upright and gesturing for Tuck to follow him as he slowly made his way down a section of the ridge that wasn't as steep as the rest of it. Even so, the snow made it impossible to walk with any degree of control and he found himself falling onto his backside before momentum carried him the rest of the way down and he rolled into the campsite with as much grace as a drunk with a broken leg.

Tuck suffered the same fate, falling, rolling, and crashing into John just as the bailiff regained his feet. At any other time they'd both have laughed, but they did not even smile as they hastily got to their feet, mud and wet snow clinging to them as they clutched their quarterstaffs and stared about at the seemingly deserted camp.

"There's no one here," Tuck said at last, huge disappointment evident in his tone.

John said nothing, wondering if he'd brought them there for naught. Where the hell was Will Scarlet? If he wasn't here, why had John seen those trees in his otherworldly vision? Then he remembered the hole that he'd seen in that vision and looked about for it.

"There!" he cried, spotting the gaping dark void just a few feet away from them. "In there, Tuck, help me."

They ran across and knelt beside the hole, peering into it. "Will!" John called down, but there was no reply. "Scarlet! Are you down there, you ugly turd?"

"I can't see a thing," Tuck muttered, eyes straining. "Where did this hole even come from? I don't remember it being here before."

John shook his head in exasperation. "I don't know, does it matter? Maybe the men that were camping out here dug it to hide stolen goods. Or maybe it's a sink hole that just opened up for no reason one day. Who cares?"

Tuck had wandered off and the sound of flint striking steel came to John. The friar had taken out his little pouch of kindling and, using the wood that was already in the extinguished fire, very quickly had a fresh blaze going.

"Move back," Tuck said, carrying a burning stick across to the hole and holding it over the top. They peered down, praying they would see Tuck, but even with the light from the fire it was hard to make anything out.

"He's there!" John finally exploded. "My vision was right! I see his hair. He must be sitting up, but…unconscious." He didn't look at Tuck and was glad the friar didn't say what they were both thinking. If Will *was* down that hole and not moving or making a sound, it was highly likely he wasn't simply unconscious. In this cold, he would be dead.

"You'll have to go down," Tuck said.

"Me? Why can't you go?"

"I'm too wide," the friar replied, hurrying away and searching the ground. "And you're taller so you don't have as far to fall. Go, John, time is of the essence. I'll find a long branch you can use to climb back out."

"Climb back out? While carrying Will?" John gaped at Tuck as if he'd gone mad.

"First, we need to make sure he's alright. Now, go, John, before it's too late!"

Muttering terrible, un-Christmas-like oaths, John heaved a great sigh and sat down on the edge of the hole. "God save us," he said, and then spun on his backside and used his arms to lower himself down gently into the gloom.

"Is he there?" Tuck demanded, forgetting his branch-hunting duties for a moment and looking down at John.

The bailiff was crouching, staring silently at what he'd taken for Will's hair.

"Is it him?" Tuck cried. "Why are you just sitting there, by God? Is he alive?"

"Bring that burning stick back over, Tuck, and stop shouting," John called up. "Hurry."

A moment later the interior of the hole was lit by flickering orange firelight and John was standing up, great arms cradling the victim they'd come there to rescue.

FIVE

"That's not Will," Tuck said, dumbfounded.

"Thanks for letting me know," John retorted sarcastically. "I wasn't sure." His words were acid, but his tone was gentle so as not to cause any more fright to the already terrified, shocked bundle he'd found in the hole.

It was Will Scarlet's dog, Mite.

"Get that branch, Tuck," commanded the bailiff. "This poor little thing is freezing and terrified."

While he waited for the friar to find something big enough, and strong enough to take his weight, John wrapped the end of his cloak about the shivering dog and held it in close, sharing his body heat. The dog was alive, and seemed to be in one piece with no obvious injuries, but he'd either fallen or been thrown into that hole after being witness to God knew what and the whole ordeal had terrified him. "We'll take care of you," John murmured soothingly, stroking the dog's ears. "You're safe now, little one."

It took a while but, at last, Friar Tuck returned with a thick, straight log about four feet long. When John propped it up at an angle against the wall of the hole it was just enough for him to reach up and hand Mite to Tuck, before clambering out himself.

The anxious dog did not attempt to run away, or even jump out of Tuck's arms as he took a seat on the ground by the fire. John came and flopped down beside them, exhausted from the day's efforts.

"What do we do now?" Tuck asked. "Will was obviously here at one point, and led you here with that blasphemous mind connection thing you two seem to share, but he's not now."

John stared at the dancing flames, almost entranced by their movement. All he wanted to do at that moment was rest, and then, perhaps, have something to eat and drink for he'd not eaten anything since the baker's honey cake hours ago and he was starting to feel shaky.

"Let's get warm," the bailiff said at last, tearing his gaze away from the crackling fire. "Let Mite get over his scare."

"And then?"

"And then we'll continue the hunt for Scarlet."

"In the dark?" Tuck asked quietly, and with little enthusiasm.

John didn't reply. There was no need. It didn't matter how dark it got, or how cold – their friend was in trouble and they would search until they found him.

SIX

It had been bitterly cold during the day, so John was worried the night would be unbearable as they resumed the hunt for Will Scarlet, but the wind had died down and, since it was no longer snowing, they were more comfortable as they walked. The fire, and some well-earned food, had warmed them all both inside and out, and even Mite appeared happier.

"We might not have found Will yet," Tuck said, his hood staying up now, making him considerably less grumpy than earlier. "But Mite seems to have his scent."

It was true, the little brown terrier was proving a Godsend, for he was leading the way, following the course of the nearby stream closely, in such a way that it was clear he knew where he was going. Of course, the dog might simply have caught the scent of a deer or a rabbit, but the men had no choice but to follow.

John had borrowed the rope Tuck used to keep his grey cassock tight around his waist to fashion a lead for the hound. If they stumbled across the outlaws who were somewhere nearby, they didn't want the dog giving them away.

It was hard to tell what time it was, for the clouds obscured most of the sky, but with the glimpses they did manage to get of the stars John thought it was close to midnight when they heard, a short distance ahead, raised voices.

Immediately, both men halted, and John lifted Mite, holding the dog close, ready to clamp its muzzle shut should it start barking. Mite had been trained by Will to hunt though, and made no sound as they listened.

They'd lost track of the stream a while ago, but it – or perhaps a different one – was beside them now, carving its glittering path through the dark, frozen landscape. It sounded as though there were men ahead, and the presence of the water supply would, as before, provide a good location for a camp. Why else would there be men out here in the wilderness in the middle of the night, if they were not sheltering there? It had to be a camp.

Slowly, silently, John led Tuck on, senses straining for signs of lookouts. Whoever was talking was making no effort to be quiet, though, suggesting they'd also not have bothered posting a watch. Either they were too arrogant, or too stupid, to expect trouble.

As outlaws, John and Tuck had soon learned that danger was never far away, be it from the sheriff's soldiers, or some other group of criminals living in the forest and eager for plunder.

"Stay here, lad," John murmured, tethering Mite's leash to a sapling. "We'll be back soon." He petted the dog, smiling reassuringly. "You be good, alright?"

"How d'you want to do this?" Tuck asked, gazing in the direction of the camp. "It sounds like there's at least two men there. Perhaps more, if some are asleep."

John thought about it. They could deal with two enemies without trouble, he was sure of that. God, he could defeat two men himself, and Tuck was no slouch when it came to a fight. Still, the friar was right, it was possible there were more men in the camp than they could hear. He shrugged. Cunning plans had never been John's thing.

"You go to the left, I'll go to the right. If there's only a handful of them, and they're looking for trouble, we give it to them. Right?"

Tuck grinned, nodding enthusiastically. "I like it."

"Give me enough time to get in position, and then you wander into their camp playing the part of the lost friar. If you need me, I'll be there."

"God protect us," Tuck said, blessing himself and grasping John's wrist in farewell. "Take care, my friend," he said, and then he'd disappeared into the night, swallowed by its black embrace.

The giant bailiff turned in the other direction and started to move, taking care to make no sound as he went which wasn't too hard as anything that might have given him away, such as a dry twig, was covered by hard packed snow. It would hardly matter even if he'd snapped a dozen brittle twigs anyway, he thought, for whoever was camped ahead was talking as loudly as if they were safe and snug in a tavern. If these were outlaws, they wouldn't survive long, thought the bailiff as he took up a position behind a hawthorn bush.

A fire blazed merrily in front of him, beside the stream. By the fire's light he could see two men, hunched over as they laughed and joked. Their conversation confirmed their status as outlaws, for they were discussing thefts they'd committed, and how they'd evaded some foresters that morning. There were shelters constructed against four of the trees beside their fire, much like the ones John had seen at the camp where they'd found Mite.

There was no sign of Will Scarlet.

John could not decide if that was a good or a bad thing, but he didn't have long to think on it, for the tonsured head of Friar Tuck suddenly appeared, framed in the firelight, his familiar jovial smile playing across his round face.

The two men beside the fire cried out in alarm and jumped to their feet. John cursed silently as he saw the glint of steel blades in the light from the flames.

Should John move now, before Tuck was beset by the armed men? Or give the friar time to talk to them and, hopefully, set them at ease?

"My children!" Tuck was already speaking so John decided to give him a chance to discover what he could.

The men looked at one another in confusion, and then another scruffy-looking individual came stumbling out from beneath one of the shelters, wrapped in bulky furs and appearing as if he'd not had a wash in months. He seemed to have been drunk for a similar length of time and he gaped at Friar Tuck as if Jesus Christ himself had wandered into their camp on Christmas Eve.

"My children," Tuck was saying, smiling, hands spread wide as if addressing the congregation in St Mary's. "It's a miracle I stumbled upon your camp!"

"Who the hell are you," one of the men demanded, hand on something John couldn't make out at his waist. "How the hell did you get here, in this weather?"

"I'm a wandering friar," said Tuck, walking across and warming his hands by the fire, still beaming merrily. "I was robbed by some outlaws a few miles back, however, and they stole all my supplies. With no way to make a fire, and no food, I thought I might die. I prayed to God, and he led me here, to you. You men have saved my life!"

There was a sudden loud mumbling and a thumping sound and John's eyes snapped to one of the crude shelters. Now he could see someone's feet, tied at the ankles and hitting against the ground. John couldn't see the person's face, but they were clearly being held prisoner by the three men. Was it Will? It was too dark to see, despite the campfire.

"We're not your saviours, friar," the drunk man slurred, pulling a knife from his belt and showing it to Tuck. The blade was in poor condition and so dirty that it barely even reflected the firelight, but even a poorly maintained knife could kill. "Be on your way," the drunk went on, and his two companions flanked him now, all three in a row, staring down Tuck.

"But I'll die out there," Tuck cried as if he were terrified. "It's Christmas. Would you turn a man of God away on such a night? Are you monsters?"

The drunk, who appeared to be the leader of the group, was clearly uncertain but he brandished his knife again. "It's none of your business who or what we are. We've nothing to share with you, we barely even have food for ourselves, so leave."

John had seen enough, and he stepped out from behind the hawthorn bush, walking forward into the light. He made no attempt to move silently and all three of the outlaws turned at his approach. If they'd been surprised by Tuck's sudden appearance, the sight of the biggest man they'd ever seen wandering into their camp must have been a terrific shock.

The drunk acted on instinct, charging at John and swinging wildly with his dirty knife. Unfortunately for him, he was too inebriated to judge distances properly and his blade whistled harmlessly through the air before the butt of John's quarterstaff came around and cracked him across the side of the head.

"I know you!" one of the other two men shouted, backing away from John, eyes wide in fright. "You're that wolf's head."

"I thought *you* were the wolf's head," John replied, moving forward, quarterstaff held menacingly before him. "Who's that you've got trussed up like a Christmas goose in the shelter there?"

The man stammered a reply, but he'd forgotten Tuck. The friar had taken out the cudgel he'd carried with him for decades – the very same one he'd used to knock Adam Bell out cold in Barnsdale years before. He hit the unsuspecting man across the back of the head with it now, dropping him senseless to the frozen ground.

Only one man remained, and he had no heart for a fight.

"Throw down any weapons you have," John commanded, his voice heavy with the threat of violence.

The final outlaw did as he was told immediately, dropping a short knife and then spreading his arms to show he was not a danger to them.

"Free their prisoner," John said to Tuck and the friar hurried to do so, lifting the outlaw's knife as he passed and using that to cut the bonds that held the captive. It was Will Scarlet, and, when his hands were free he pulled down the rope that had been tied around his mouth to keep him quiet and released a stream of curses and oaths so extreme that Tuck bowed his head and made the sign of the cross.

Before the circulation could return to his limbs and he was able to attack the three men who'd tied him up, a little brown shape tore through the camp, jumping at Scarlet's face with excited yelps and whimpers.

"Mite!" Will laughed, rage momentarily forgotten as his face was licked repeatedly and he was forced to fend off the terrier's affections. "I thought you were dead!"

"He would have been," Tuck told him. "If we hadn't found him. Oh, would you look at that, he's chewed right through my belt, that's how he's got free! By the body and blood of Christ, Will, what's been going on out here?"

"Let him gather himself before he tells us," John said. "Come and get heated up by the fire, Scarlet. Have some of the food and drink these wolf's heads have got lying about. They weren't lying though – they've not got much at all."

Tuck threw him the three sections of rope that had been used to bind Will's hands, legs, and mouth, and he took them now to tie up the outlaws who offered no resistance whatsoever, which was a wise move on their part.

For a while, the camp was quiet, apart from Will's muttered complaints and threats aimed at his captors, but, when he was seated by the fire and furnished with some ale and small cuts of rabbit that the outlaws had been roasting on a spit, even he quietened down. He chewed like a man who hadn't eaten in a week, although he did share some of the gristly parts of the rabbit with Mite who appeared to be fully over his own ordeal now.

Tuck and John were almost as glad as Will to get some food and drink and warm their bones by the fire for it had been an exciting night, but a long, exhausting one too.

So exhausting that by the time they'd finished eating and John and Tuck were ready to hear Will's tale, they noticed he was lying on his side, snoring loudly, with Mite cuddled in against his chest, also fast asleep.

"By all the saints, we do all the work to rescue him, then he's the one that gets to sleep while we're left on watch," John growled, but he was smiling, just happy that everything had turned out well in the end, and they were all alive and uninjured.

The clouds parted overhead and Tuck looked up, admiring the stars.

"We've been out in this all day," John noted. "It's past midnight."

"It is," Tuck agreed cheerily. "Merry Christmas, John! And a Merry Christmas to all." He turned to the three captive outlaws with a beatific smile, but, from the muttered oaths they returned in his direction, they did not share in Tuck's joy for Christ's special day.

SEVEN

The journey back to Wakefield was nowhere near as hard or as stressful for John and Tuck as the previous day's had been. Will slept all through the night, while the bailiff and the friar took turns on watch. All three felt quite rested when they awoke, being used to sleeping deeply whenever they got the chance, even now, so many years after their days as wolf's heads were behind them.

The three outlaws who'd taken Will prisoner were quiet and more frightened than sullen and, since they couldn't just let them go until they knew who they were, John took them back to Wakefield. Mite bounded along at their feet, like a shepherd's dog, making sure they didn't stray from the pack as they walked through the snowy fields back to town.

It was a crisp, dry morning, not windy, and the sun even came up to guide them homewards. Truly, it was a blessed morning.

Well, unless you were one of the three outlaws.

"Are you going to tell us what happened yesterday, Scarlet?" John had asked as soon as the journey began.

"No," Will replied. "I'd just need to repeat myself when we get to Wakefield. So I'll save my story until we're there, in St Mary's, nice and cosy, and I've got a cup or three of wassail down my neck."

That was his final word on it and he wouldn't change his mind, despite John and Tuck's demands, so they walked across the fields mostly in silence, heading for Scarlet's steadings in case Elspeth and Blase had returned there.

It didn't take too long to reach the farm – they'd been closer to it than any of them had realised – but it was deserted, apart from Holdfast who was glad to see his master, and his little companion, Mite. The reunited dogs were fed and watered and then left safely locked within the house as John, Tuck, and Will took their horses from the stables and rode for town with the three prisoners tethered behind them on foot.

Since Will wouldn't tell them anything about the previous day's events, John had no idea what the prisoners had done, what they were capable of, or why they were running from the law. The fact that Scarlet had not given any of them a good beating spoke volumes, however...

"What are you going to do with us?" their scruffy leader, who had by now completely sobered up, asked nervously as the town buildings came into sight and the bell of St Mary's rang out across the countryside proclaiming Christ's birth.

"I don't know yet," John replied. "I don't know what you've done!"

"You were an outlaw," the man said. "You know what it's like. You know how easy it is to get on the wrong side of a crooked bailiff."

John turned in his saddle and looked at the man, who he had to admit spoke the truth. "We'll know soon enough what's to be done with you," he said. "We're nearly there."

A crowd of children had spotted their approach and began to crowd around them now. "Hey," John called down to them. "Go to my house and bring my wife, and anyone else that's there, to the church. All right? A farthing to whoever gets there first!"

The boys and girls sprinted off, screaming and jostling one another in their haste to earn the money. A farthing was a fortune to a child, and more than any could expect even on Christmas Day.

The town headman appeared then, striding out into the narrow, muddy street and staring at the riders and their captives. He did not look terribly surprised by what he was seeing, for John and his friends were often involved in strange situations with strange people. He did ask what was happening, however, and was happy to take the three outlaws into custody, calling a few of the younger, bigger, local men to assist him. They led the men behind as John, Tuck, and Will continued to St Mary's.

With it being Christmas Day the church was busy and would remain so into the night. Already the priest, Father Myrc, had said Mass, but now, as it approached mid-morning, tables and benches were being setup, ready for food and drink to be laid out for those who would come and enjoy the festivities there. Carols would be sung, games played, stories told, perhaps even a play, and through it all the people of Wakefield would enjoy much ale, wassail, and better food than they'd enjoyed for a long time.

Word of the three former outlaws riding into town with another three wolf's heads had quickly spread, and people began flocking to St Mary's to enjoy the excitement. Amber arrived soon, running into the building with Elspeth and Blase in tow, and the two wives enjoyed happy reunions with their husbands, while Tuck stood by smiling and rubbing his belly at the sight of all the food being placed on the tables around him.

"Where the hell have you all been?" Amber demanded. "When you didn't come home last night we feared you'd been killed!"

"Killed? Me?" John asked, eyebrows raised. "Who could kill me?"

"I bloody will if you ever disappear like that again, you big oaf," Amber retorted, but it was hard to be angry at Little John for long and her frown quickly turned into a smile.

Elspeth was not so easily mollified, demanding answers from Will and berating him loudly for chasing after the outlaws alone in the first place.

"It's time you told us all what happened to you yesterday," Tuck said, his rich, powerful voice filling the church and drawing excited nods from the people gathered there.

"All right," Will agreed. "But it's not a very long, or exciting tale."

"Just get on with it," Elspeth commanded, folding her arms and tilting her head to one side.

"Well, I saw those three scruffy bastards hanging about near my barn," he said. "It was obvious they were up to no good. I watched them for a bit, and saw them lifting one of my hens and walking off with it. I went after them but they killed the bird before I could catch up to them."

"It was making a lot of noise," Elspeth said.

"Exactly," Will nodded. "That's why they killed it. And that's when I told you I was going after them and to lock the door until I came home."

"But you never did!"

"They ran away from me," Will said. "When they saw me coming after them with my dogs, they didn't have the balls to stand and fight. Three of them, against one, yet they ran away." He shook his head with a disgusted laugh. "They don't make outlaws like us any more," he told John and Tuck, who both murmured in agreement.

"Just as bloody well," Amber said. "Or you'd be dead now."

"Probably," Will admitted ruefully. "But they ran, and I chased them, taking my dogs with me. They ran for a long time. I must admit, I'm not quite as fit as I used to be and they lost me, but Holdfast was able to track them. It started to snow though, and Holdfast didn't deal with it too well. He was shivering and frightened so I sent him home."

"That just scared me even more," Elspeth said. "When the dog came home without you."

Will nodded apologetically and went on with his tale. "Mite led me on. He's a hardy little thing. The snow started to get really heavy then, though, and I lost sight of him. He must have caught the scent of the bastards somewhere close and went after them himself."

"He's as daft as his master," Elspeth grumbled, drawing laughs from the villagers gathered about. Even Father Myrc was grinning.

"Then what?" John asked. "Did you find them and get into a fight?"

Will frowned and reached up to touch the back of his head. "No. I don't really know what happened next. One moment I was walking through the snow, slipping about, and the next thing I knew I was tied up and lying in the outlaws' camp where you found me."

John and Tuck shared a look. That was it? They'd assumed Will had attacked the three men and been overpowered.

"Not a very exciting story," an old woman in the crowd piped up. "I was hoping to hear something with more action and adventure in it."

"I was expecting there to be a lot more fighting in it," someone else said. "Usually Will Scarlet likes to get into fights."

"Well, there was a fight," John said defensively, feeling somehow as if he and his friends were being slighted. "Me and Tuck knocked a couple of the outlaws out."

"I was roaring drunk," the scruffy outlaw leader called out. "Anyone could have knocked me out."

"You're sober now," John retorted. "You want me to do it again?"

"Aye, do it, John," the old woman cackled. "We don't want any outlaws near Wakefield."

"What about them?" the scruffy wolf's head demanded, pointing at John, Tuck and Will. "They were outlaws, and you all loved them. Everyone in England knows the stories!"

"They were alright though," said the tavern keeper, Alexander. "The rest of you are a bunch of bastards."

"What's your name?" Elspeth asked the outlaw leader. "Why didn't you kill my husband? And how did he end up at your camp?"

"My name is Simon. I saw your man slip and fall," he replied. "We were hiding from him when he took a tumble. Cracked his head off a rock that was underneath the snow. We couldn't just leave him there in that weather, he'd have died."

John was frowning. "So you saved his life? But why tie him up and cart him away to your new camp?"

"We had to tie him up," Simon replied as if John was stupid. "He was bloody furious at us for stealing his hen. He'd have killed us if we didn't tie him up." He shrugged. "And, like I said, he was unconscious. We couldn't just leave him there in the middle of nowhere to die. So we carried him on a makeshift stretcher all the way to our new camp, where you and the fat friar attacked us."

"What about the dog?" John asked.

"Crazy little bastard came charging at us when we were putting him onto the stretcher," the outlaw replied, nodding towards Will. "That dog is a demon! It attacked me, biting my feet and stuff, but it didn't notice the big hole and fell in."

"You left it there?"

"Would you have tried to get it out?"

John had to admit that he probably wouldn't, given the fact that Mite had been trying to kill them, and they were already dealing with the unconscious Will Scarlet.

"Why are you outlaws at all?" Tuck asked. "What's made you so desperate that you're reduced to stealing hens from farms?"

Simon sighed, but the look of sadness that had been on his face was soon replaced by one of anger. "The bailiff in Rotherham," he growled. "We are, were, traders there. Doing well too. But the bailiff, Roger Attemill, decided he wanted a cut of our profits. Threatened to burn down our warehouse if we didn't pay him to 'look after it'. We refused, and the next thing we knew the warehouse, with all our stock in it, had been set alight and the bailiff had witnesses who said we'd been seen setting the fires."

Tuck gave a low whistle. Everyone knew how seriously fire was taken in a town – with the buildings packed close together, and made mostly from materials like wood and thatch, even a small fire could quickly spread and become a raging inferno that killed and destroyed everything in its wake.

"We couldn't let them arrest us, could we? You all know how things would have turned out for us. We'd have been torn apart by the mob that bastard bailiff had stirred up. We were lucky to escape into the forest and we've been running ever since." He shrugged with a sad smile. "We're not very good woodsmen. It's been hard."

"We've been forced to become the criminals the bailiff said we were," one of the other outlaws added.

"Lost everything so we have," the third nodded. "And now, you'll send us back to Rotherham and that'll be it."

The three men were utterly dejected and their gloomy words were met with silence by those villagers who'd managed to cram into St Mary's. The sombre atmosphere was not in keeping with the spirit of the day at all.

"Maybe not," said John.

"What d'you mean?" asked Simon.

"I know that bailiff you mentioned, Roger Attemill. The man's an arrogant arsehole, and I know the sheriff has long suspected he was crooked. This could be just what Sir Henry needs to prove it, and have the man removed from his post."

"That would mean you three would be off the hook," Tuck said, beaming again.

The outlaws gaped at them, open mouthed, desperate to believe them but afraid to.

"That would truly be a Christmas miracle," muttered Simon, and Father Myrc laughed.

"That is exactly what these gentlemen seem to deliver every year around this time! It's become something of a habit."

"Well then," said Will, putting an arm around his wife and son and grinning broadly. "If that's all done with, let's get those three untied, and someone pour the wassail! It's Christmas!"

The church erupted in cheers and everyone began pouring drinks, laying out food, wishing one another the compliments of the day, and some even struck up a carol. With the holly and ivy colouring the place with green leaves and red berries, and a tree in the corner bedecked with apples and gingerbread, it was a wonderfully festive scene, especially when the snow started to fall once more outside.

Tuck wandered about the room, searching for tasty morsels the villagers had brought in for their fellows to share, while John and Will stood with their wives and young Blase, filling them in on what had transpired over the last twenty-four hours in more detail.

"What I don't understand," said Elspeth, biting into a slice of Amber's cheese tart which the two women had baked together the day before. "Is how you and Tuck actually found Will at all. What led you in the right direction?"

John smiled proudly and put his arm around Will in a rough hug. "We have a connection, me and Will," he pronounced, tapping first his head, and then his friend's. "We discovered it at the tavern the other night, I told you about it Amber."

His wife's face twisted in a cynical frown.

"It's true," John protested. "I just tried to picture the place where Will was in my mind, and he must have sent the image of it to me. Three trees, with the hole we found Mite in. I recognised it immediately as our old camp."

Will was frowning even harder than Amber and he stepped back, staring at John. "But I was never at that old camp, John," he said. "Not awake anyway. Remember, I fell and knocked myself out before I reached it. The outlaws carried me there when I was out cold, and then carried me across the fields to their new camp." He bit into his own slice of the cheese tart, crumbs tumbling from his mouth as he finished, "So you can't have had any connection with me to lead you there, John."

They stood in thoughtful silence then, eating and drinking.

"Well, something led me to Mite," John said at last, and then he paused, realisation dawning on him. At the same time, Will was reaching the same conclusion as his big friend.

It had been the dog that John had the connection with, not Will Scarlet!

"Mite was there at the tavern the night we were playing the blindfold game," Will burst out, a huge grin on his face. "Sitting right there on my lap for most of the time."

Amber and Elspeth looked at one another, frowns changing to amusement as they too began to understand what had happened.

"I always said you were about as smart as a dog, John," cackled Tuck, appearing behind the bailiff and stealing some of the tart from his hand. "But I never realised you were *actually* a dog! Still, dogs are God's creatures, just like us."

For once, Little John was absolutely speechless.

"Dog or not, all's turned out for the best," said Amber. "The outlaws should get their lives back, with John's help, and Will is home safely again."

"As is Mite," Tuck added, winking at John who was still too shocked to respond with even a crude gesture.

"To you, John," said Will, raising his cup of wassail in the air and grinning at the bailiff as everyone nearby joined in with the toast. "To you, and your strange connection with farm animals!"

Little John had finally got over his surprise and even he was laughing now, for it truly had been a miracle that brought them all safely together in St Mary's that Christmas Day.

"To me," he shouted, hoisting his own cup aloft. "And a merry Christmas one and all!"

THE END

AUTHOR'S NOTE

Well, I hope you enjoyed another Christmas tale! I wasn't planning on writing one this year – <u>The Heathen Horde</u> was published not long ago and my publishers weren't sure it would be a good idea for me to put out a novella so soon afterwards, in case it took focus/sales away from the novel. I can see their point, and I dearly want *The Heathen Horde* to be a success, so I agreed not to do a winter story on Kindle in 2023.

But it's a tradition now, isn't it? For me, and for some of you, who tell me that you really look forward to joining Tuck, Will, and Little John for a snowy adventure. I even listen to *Friar Tuck and the Christmas Devil* on Audible every year! So, when I had a spare few days I decided I'd write a short story of about 5,000 words and just give it away for free to everyone subscribed to my Email List. A Christmas gift to thank my subscribers for their continued support.

I'm not sure where the idea for the story came from. There was an episode of 60's classic TV show THE PRISONER which had Number 6 forming a psychic connection with one of Number 2's nefarious minions, but she was human, not canine! Poor John will probably be mocked for years to come over his mental link with Will's dog. I thought it was a fun little twist that fitted perfectly with a winter tale like this.

I soon passed my 5,000-word target for the story, of course, and it's ended up being over 12,000 words long – a novelette! A decent freebie, I hope. Maybe I will publish it properly on Kindle next year, along with another new winter story but, for now, I really hope *The Christmas Hunt* brought you some cheer and got you into the spirit of the season.

Going forward I still have to write a third book in my Alfred the Great series (book 2 was completed before I wrote this novelette), and then it will be back to the adventures of Bellicus and Duro with a sixth novel in the Warrior Druid of Britain Chronicles. I'm looking forward to seeing what trouble they get into next!

I hope you all have a fantastic Christmas and a brilliant 2024. If you would like to spread good cheer my way, it would be great if you'd leave a 5 star review for any of my books you've read, and check out the podcast I do with Matthew Harffy, <u>Rock, Paper, Swords! The Historical Action & Adventure Podcast</u>. If you want to keep enjoying the festive spirit, check out the song we've just released on all streaming platforms like Spotify and iTunes – it's called "Christmas is Coming" and it rocks hard, I think.

Cheers!

Steven A. McKay,
Old Kilpatrick,
3 November 2023

ALSO BY STEVEN A. MCKAY

& ACKNOWLEDGEMENTS

The Forest Lord Series:
Wolf's Head
The Wolf and the Raven
Rise of the Wolf
Blood of the Wolf

Knight of the Cross*
Friar Tuck and the Christmas Devil*
The Prisoner*
The Escape*
The Abbey of Death*
Faces of Darkness*
Sworn To God
The House In The Marsh*
The Pedlar's Promise*

The Warrior Druid of Britain Chronicles
The Druid
Song of the Centurion
The Northern Throne
The Bear of Britain
Over The Wall*
Wrath of the Picts
The Vengeance of Merlin

LUCIA – A Roman Slave's Tale

Alfred the Great trilogy

The Heathen Horde
Sword of the Saxons
King of Wessex

Titles marked * are spin-off novellas, novelettes, or short stories. All others are full length novels.

Acknowledgements

A big 'Merry Christmas!' to my beta reader,
Bernadette McDade,
and my editor, Richenda Todd!

Printed in Great Britain
by Amazon